STORM SEASON

One Storm. Three novellas.

J.T. Ellison

Alex Kava

Erica Spindler

PRAIRIE WIND PUBLISHING
OMAHA, NEBRASKA

Prairie Wind Publishing
18149 Trailridge Road
Omaha, Nebraska 68135
www.pwindpub.com

Interior design & formatting: Deb Carlin, Prairie Wind Publishing
Book cover design: Deb Carlin, Prairie Wind Publishing
Images for Cover: iPhotoStock

Ordering Information:
Quantity sales. Special discounts are available on quantity purchases by corporations, associations, and others. For details, contact Deb Carlin at the address above.

Photo Credits:
Alex Kava by Deb Carlin, Prairie Wind Publishing
J.T. Ellison by Chris Blanz, Cabedge
Erica Spinder by Hoffman Miller Advertising

ISBN:1540470679

First Edition Printing December 2016
Printed in the United States of America
10 9 8 7 6 5 4 3 2 1

DEDICATION

To J.T. Ellison, Erica Spindler and Alex Kava.
From Deb Carlin

You three "pals" have given readers a fantastic journey with all of your novels. Thank you for your twisted words. Your minds think a lot alike.

As readers, we beg that you continue your journeys...

#KeepWriting

Foreword by Deb Carlin

Ivan, Dennis, Katrina, Sandy—storms worthy of a name. Killer storms.

In July Erica, Alex, J.T. and I started brainstorming about a follow-up to SLICES OF NIGHT. The authors knew they wanted something to link all three stories again. But what? Another killer? A theme or ritual? I suppose I should back up a bit for those of you who might not be familiar with SLICES OF NIGHT and how three bestselling authors decided to collaborate on a project together. Quite honestly, it was one fan, an avid reader who loves each of their novels and decided to nag them until they wrote a novella together.

Yes, if you haven't guessed by now, that avid reader, that nag, was me. I even offered my services of organizing, managing and publishing the novella. Of course, I was warned that bringing three authors together to write one project might be like trying to herd cats. Especially three Type A personalities.

(Make that four Type A's when you add me into the mix.) But I knew what a treat the result would be for other readers like me.

In SLICES OF NIGHT one killer travels from New Orleans to Nashville then Omaha. Each author showcased her protagonist and her city while dealing with the same killer. The novella - done in three parts - also allowed readers a sampling of each author's style and technique in storytelling. It was a huge success. So much so, that the Polish edition was just published last month. And because all three authors are not just seasoned professionals, but also friends of mine, the project was a lot of fun. Not at all like herding cats.

However, success beyond all expectations is always fun. The difficulty can be following that up with an equally amazing project. But that's exactly what Erica, Alex and J.T.

have done with STORM SEASON.

Back in July during that first brainstorm teleconference one of us made note about hurricane season just getting underway. All three authors and I have experienced catastrophic storms from hurricanes and floods to ice storms and blizzards. So we understand how one storm system can affect a wide swath of the country.

We started asking what if the thread between all three stories was one massive storm system—one that stretched from the Midwest down to the Panhandle of Florida and back up the eastern coast? Keep in mind this was in July 2012 before Hurricane Sandy devastated an entire section of the country with everything from ice and snow to flooding and damaging winds. Yes, it's a bit unnerving to listen to authors dreaming up things before they happen.

With the storm as the tie-in, each author, once again, could showcase her protagonist as well as her own storytelling style. In follow-up emails, Erica started calling the project STORM SEASON and soon we couldn't imagine it being called anything else.

SLICES OF NIGHT was one novella in three parts. STORM SEASON is twice as long and is three novellas with one killer storm. Each is an amazing story on its own. Together they are STORM SEASON – another superb treat for readers. I know you will enjoy it as much as I have.

Table of Contents

STORM SEASON

One Storm. Three novellas.

STORM SEASON—ONE STORM. THREE NOVELLAS.
ERICA SPINDLER
DEEP FREEZE
ROCKFORD, ILLINOIS

Rockford, Illinois
7:40 a.m.

"Anybody else notice it's the end of the frickin' world?"

Violent Crimes Bureau Detective Mary Catherine Riggio, crouched beside the dead girl, glanced up.

The question came from Nick Sorenstein, one of the ID guys. Their resident doomsday prophet. Today the end was coming via the effects of global warming.

"It certainly is for this girl," she said.

A jogger had spotted the vic about an hour ago, half in and half out of the water. In an effort to "save" her, he'd hauled her out and turned her over. Then promptly tossed his cookies.

"You keeping up with the weather, Riggio? You aware that yet another "freak—" he made quotation marks with his fingers "—storm's moving in?"

"Yeah, I noticed. It's cold, then hot, then cold again. I never know whether I should wear my black jacket or my black jacket."

Sorenstein snorted, not amused. "Your global view's about the circumference of a dime."

"Not at all." She indicated a circle around the victim. "Right now, I'd say it's about ten feet."

"Time to wake up. We keep fucking with Mother Nature, we'll end up like the dinosaurs. Extinct."

Jackson, one of the crime scene techs, laughed. "Sorenstein, buddy, you off your meds?"

"Screw you, man. I'm not gonna end up like T-Rex. Adapt, man. Adapt or die." Jackson laughed again, and Nick scowled. "Just shut up and take your little pictures."

Jackson pointed the Nikon at him and snapped a shot. "Works of art, asshole."

M.C. forced their bickering out of her head and focused on the young woman. Long brown hair, wet and matted. Face scraped and muddy. Eyes open. Other than her face, no outward signs of trauma.

Her partner arrived. Kitt Lundgren, mentor, partner, and best friend. They had been through some seriously twisted shit together.

"What's Sorenstein's problem?" she asked, squatting beside M.C.

"Either the end of the world's here, or he's off his meds."

Kitt grinned. "I know Sorenstein and I've seen the weather report, so I'm thinking we've got a fifty-fifty shot at both." She indicated the vic. "What's her story?"

"Jogger found her face-down in the water. She probably got herself good and juiced, ended up in the water and—"

"Say goodnight, Gracie." Kitt nodded. "Wha'd'ya think? Drugs or alcohol?"

"Toxicology will tell the tale."

"Hello, Detectives."

Frances Roselli, coroner's chief pathologist. As far as M.C. was concerned, the man was a freaking genius.

"Goody," Kitt said. "The gang's all here."

He fitted on gloves. "Either of you see this morning's weather report?"

M.C. rolled her eyes. "Not you, too, Roselli."

"Jim Cantore's butt is already parked in Madison, Wisconsin."

"Our cheese-loving friends up north must be Ground Zero," Kitt said.

"Seems to me *this* is Ground Zero," M.C. snapped. "Could we get to it?"

He knelt down beside them. "You're a little cranky this morning, Detective. Anything I can help with?"

"Just don't have the patience for this whole 'world's coming to an end' thing. We've got a job, let's work it."

"Right you are." Frances cleared his throat. "This young lady have a name?"

"Whitney Bello. Twenty-three years old. Rock Valley student. ID was in her wallet. Also twenty dollars."

He nodded. "Give me a few minutes with Ms. Bello. I'll see what she has to say."

M.C. and Kitt stood. The Rock River Recreation path ran along the east side of the river and meandered through the city. This particular spot fell behind the Ice House, home of the IceHogs, Rockford's AHL team.

The parking lot was empty save for one vehicle, a small sport utility vehicle. They started for it.

"Since when does Sorenstein's craziness get under your skin?" Kitt asked.

M.C. let out a long breath. She could dodge the question with an evasion, but Kitt knew her too well for that. "Erik asked me again. Last night."

"And you said no."

Her response was neither a question nor a judgment. M.C. responded as if it were both. "I'm not ready. It's too soon."

"Three years."

"Thanks for counting."

"Just keeping it real, partner." Kitt paused, then looked at her. "I think Dan would want you to be happy. Both of you."

"I don't want to talk about this."

To her credit, Kitt let it drop. They reached the SUV. A Ford Escape, pretty dinged up. A Rock Valley College parking sticker on the windshield.

M.C. peered in the driver's-side window. It definitely belonged to a female. A pink disaster. Clothes and boots. Backpack open, books, papers and notebooks spilling out. A half-dozen take-out coffee cups, a yoga mat. A good bit of light-colored dog fur in the backseat.

"Looks like our vic's vehicle."

Kitt nodded. "If she lived alone, Fido's going to need a trip to the nearest tree."

M.C. walked around the car, scanning the area. Nothing jumped out at her. "I'm thinking drugs. She meets her connection here, makes a buy and uses."

"Maybe it's bad stuff?"

"Then we've got a whole other problem."

They returned to the pathologist. The body handlers were preparing to transfer Bello to the morgue.

Frances signaled them to wait.

"Take a look, Detectives." He inched up the sleeve of Bello's jacket. She wore a watch, one of those flashy, fashion pieces young women were wearing. The face was cracked; the time had stopped at 12:42 a.m. "Voila. Time of death."

"Too bad all our vics aren't so considerate," Kitt said.

"Her hands are interesting as well." He carefully manipulated the right, then left. The fingertips were raw, dirt and vegetation packed under her nails.

She had been clawing at the river bottom.

"It means she was alive when she toppled in," Kitt said. "And that she tried to claw her way out."

"Exactly."

M.C. frowned. The bank wasn't steep, and free of both snow and ice, not slippery either. Just a nice, downy cover of grass. "What stopped her?"

"Probably loaded." Frances stepped away from the body and motioned the handlers to continue.

"Sad, but it happens all the time."

"Could she have had some help?" M.C. asked.

Kitt drew her eyebrows together. "Falling in? Or staying down?"

"Either. Both."

Kitt glanced at him. "What do you think, Frances?"

"From what I've seen so far, possible but not likely."

"You'll get back to us ASAP?"

"As always. Though the weather might slow things down."

M.C. grinned. "Already making excuses?"

He laughed. "You can't fight Mother Nature, Detective. Although if there was anyone who'd try, I believe it would be you."

11:10 a.m.

Bello had lived in a third floor, east side apartment. The box-style buildings had a retro feel and judging by the worn edges, had been around for awhile.

M.C. introduced herself and Kitt to the dark-haired young woman who answered the door.

She scooped up the madly yapping terrier at her feet. "Police?"

"We're here about your roommate, Whitney Bello."

"She's not home."

"Rhonda, who's at the—" The blonde who emerged from the kitchen with a mug of tea stopped and stared.

Kitt stepped in. "Detectives Lundgren and Riggio."

"They're looking for Whitney."

"No," M.C. corrected, "we're here about her. Who are you?"

"Allison," the blonde answered. "We're Whitney's roommates."

Kitt indicated the living room. "Maybe we should sit down."

"Oh, God." Allison crossed to the couch and sat hard. "Has there been an accident or something?"

"It looks like your friend drowned."

Rhonda went white. "She's dead?"

"I'm afraid so. We're so sorry for your loss."

Rhonda sat next to Allison. They both looked stunned. The dog jumped down and came to sniff M.C.'s feet. She bent and scratched the pup behind the ears, then took the remaining chair. Kitt stood behind her.

Rhonda spoke first. "You said it . . . looks like she drowned. I don't understand . . . what does that mean?"

"She was pulled out of the river, down by the Ice House. But an official cause of death hasn't been made."

Allison started to cry, and Rhonda found her hand and clutched it. "We weren't very close, but—" she stopped, blinking furiously against the tears that flooded hers. "We advertised for a roommate. At school. She answered the ad."

"At Rock Valley?"

Allison nodded, lips trembling.

"When was that?"

"The start of this term." Rhonda drew in a ragged breath. "She kept to herself."

"But she loved Max," Allison added.

M.C. looked at Allison. "Max?"

She pointed to the dog. "She takes him to the park all the time."

Rhonda jumped in. "She's sort of a health nut."

"A health nut?"

"Always exercising. Running. Yoga. Eating good stuff."

"Fruits and veggies." Allison made a face. "Brown bread."

That didn't fit the profile of a drug abuser.

"She was a student?"

"Yeah. Part-time. And she worked part-time."

"Where'd she work?"

"A counseling center." Rhonda looked at her roommate. "What was the name?"

"Kids in Crisis," Allison answered, sniffling.

She'd worked for Erik.

The strangest sensation came over M.C. Part awareness,

part dread. One of those weird moments in life that changed everything.

"That's right." Rhonda nodded. "Sometimes she called it KIC."

"She was crazy about her boss. Talked about him all the time."

M.C. had noticed how good he was to his staff, how they responded to him. Still, hearing this pretty young woman had talked about him all the time felt odd.

Kitt jumped in. "I thought she kept to herself?"

"She did, but when she was around she either talked about her job or her boyfriend, Brad."

"The boyfriend. You have a last name?"

They looked at one another and simultaneously shook their heads. "He must've had his own place, because she never brought him here."

"He a student?"

Rhonda answered. "I don't know. Do you, Alli?"

The other girl shook her head. "He might have been older. Not ancient but . . . older. I don't know why, but I got that impression."

"Me, too."

"Any idea if and where he worked?"

"Sorry." Rhonda spread her fingers. "Like I said, we—"

"Didn't know her that well," Kitt said. "Got it. One last question. Was she a drug user?"

Both women looked surprised by the question. Again, Rhonda responded first.

"Not here. We specifically advertised as a substance-free living environment. No tobacco, alcohol or drugs."

1:00 p.m.

"Hello, beautiful," Erik said to M.C. as she and Kitt stepped into his office. He kissed her, then turned to Kitt. "Good to see you, Kitt. How's Joe?"

"Fine. Busy trying to close in a build before the snow flies."

"He better hurry. According to the noon weather report, we could have two feet of it by the end of the week."

"He heard the same report and is not a happy camper. We're both hoping the weather guys are going the worst-case scenario route to boost ratings. A few flurries aren't nearly as compelling as a couple feet."

"It wouldn't be the first time." Erik turned back to M.C. and smiled. She loved the way his light eyes crinkled at the corners. He had one of those faces that was aging in all the right ways. The lines and creases complementing his face, making him more handsome rather than less. "If I'd known you were coming, we could've had lunch."

"Unfortunately, it's not a social call," Kitt said.

M.C. stepped in. "Do you have an employee named Whitney Bello?"

She saw apprehension race into his eyes. "I do. She's part-time. Why?"

M.C. and Kitt exchanged glances. He saw it and frowned. "What?"

"How well did you know her?"

"Very well. Whitney's—" he stopped, moved his gaze between them. "What's happened? Is she okay?"

"She's dead, Erik. I'm sorry."

For several moments, he simply stared at her. Then he went around his desk, pulled out the chair and sat. Heavily. As if suddenly carrying the weight of the world.

It took him a moment to collect himself and speak. "How?"

"At this point it looks like an accidental drowning."

She gave him a moment to process, then went on. "Do you know if Whitney had substance abuse issues?"

"At one time. She's been clean almost two years." He paused. "Tell me what happened."

"A jogger found her this morning, face-down in the Rock River. We don't have the pathologist's report yet, but we suspect she got juiced and either slipped or passed out."

He sighed, the sound heavy with regret. "I didn't see this coming."

"Why would you?"

"I'm not just her boss. I'm also her counselor. She started seeing me at eighteen. Court ordered appointments. She got sober, started taking classes at Rock Valley and I gave her a job. She—" he dragged his hands through his hair. "Dammit."

"What can you tell us about her?"

"She was a nice kid. Didn't have an easy childhood. Shuffled between parents who had new spouses and new families. She got lost." His throat closed over the words. He cleared it and began again. "I had no hesitation about hiring her. She was smart. Caught on quick. Worked hard."

That's what Erik specialized in—kids who had lost their way. The reasons why didn't matter; he had made it his life's mission to help them get back on track. He was so committed he'd given up the opportunity to run his family's multimillion dollar corporation, SunCorp.

"What did she do for you here?"

"She acted as a personal assistant of sorts. Ran errands for me. Shuttled things over to SunCorp headquarters. Anything I asked her to do, she did well. And with a smile."

He fell silent. Lowered his gaze. When he lifted it, the expression in his eyes was shattered. "I don't know what else to tell you."

"We talked to her roommates already. They claimed they didn't know her well. But they said she talked about a boyfriend. Brad."

"Bradley Rudd," he said. "She'd been seeing him a couple months. Really liked him."

"You don't sound so thrilled."

"I never met him. I was—" he paused. "—concerned because of his lifestyle."

"Is he a substance abuser?"

"Whitney said no. He's a bartender. Over at Spanky's. Not that there's anything inherently wrong with being a bartender but I . . . understand the lifestyle. Crazy hours. Partying. Alcohol and drugs. That wasn't where she was going."

M.C. reached across and squeezed his hand. "We don't have the pathologist's report yet, so we don't know for certain she lapsed."

"But it makes sense," Kitt said. "In terms of her drowning. We see it often."

"She's dead either way," he said softly. "I doubt a pathologist's report confirming or denying relapse is going to make it any easier."

M.C. stood. It felt wrong to leave him this way, hurting and alone.

But she had a job to do.

"I'm so sorry, Erik. I wish I could stay—"

"But you can't. I understand."

He kissed her, lingering a moment longer than was

appropriate for the situation. He drew away, searched her gaze. "You'll keep me posted?"

"Of course."

He looked at Kitt. "You're going to talk to Rudd?"

"Oh yeah. Right now."

"Heads-up, if he got her back on drugs you'll have to arrest me. Because I'll kill him. I swear I will."

His tone made M.C. believe he would do it. "I'll come by later," she said. "You'll be home?"

He said he would, and she walked away, though it took all her self-control not to turn back, hold him tightly. She left him everyday. Why so hard today? Why the sense of dread unfurling in the pit of her stomach? This sense of a clock ticking, counting down to . . . what? The end?

But the end of what? Her and Erik? Or worse?

"What's wrong?" Kitt asked as they reached her car.

M.C. looked at her, shaking off her melancholy. "Nothing. Just . . . nothing."

4:45 p.m.

Bradley Rudd wasn't what M.C. would describe as handsome. But he exuded a bad-boy charm that a lot of women gravitated to, her included. In her youth, anyway. Nothing like a whole school of hard knocks to change a girl. Make her long for something nice and steady.

As she slid onto the bar stool, M.C. flashed Rudd what she hoped was a provocative smile. He ate it right up.

"Hello, ladies," he said, setting coasters in front them both. "Looks like my afternoon just took a turn for the better."

M.C. smiled again. "I bet I could change your mind about that, stud."

"I doubt it, sugar." He grinned. "But go ahead, give it your best shot."

M.C. released a breathy little laugh. "I'll do that." She held up her shield, demeanor changing to all business. "Detective Riggio. R.P.D. My partner, Detective Lundgren."

He stared at her as if she'd sprouted horns. *Maybe I have,* M.C. thought. She was just perverse enough to enjoy the thought.

"Make that a turn for the worse, Detective. And I don't suppose you're here for a drink."

"You suppose correctly, Brad. I can call you Brad, can't I?"

"Sure." He propped against the bar, sending them a forced smile. "Call me whatever you like."

Kitt stepped in. "You know a young woman named Whitney Bello?"

He blinked. Twice. Otherwise his expression didn't alter. "Yeah, she's a friend of mine."

"A friend?"

"We go out sometimes. Why?"

"She's dead, Mr. Rudd. She died last night."

He stared at them, expression comically disbelieving. "That can't be right."

M.C. wasn't impressed. "Why's that, Brad?"

"I talked to her Sunday afternoon."

"Was that the last time you saw her?"

"No. Saturday morning. She'd spent the night."

"What time did she leave?"

"Around ten. She had a paper to write."

"Then you didn't see her again over the weekend?"

He shook his head. "Like I said, she had a paper. Plus—never mind."

"Plus what, Brad?"

"I worked all weekend. She didn't like visiting me here."

"Why was that?"

"It wasn't her kind of scene."

"Not a drinker?"

"Yeah."

"Drugs?"

M.C. had the sense that his thoughts were somewhere else. That he was wrestling with a whole other conversation in his head. She wondered who that conversation was with.

"No. No, drugs."

"You don't seem certain about that."

Again, a slack-jawed moment. *Not the sharpest tool in the shed,* M.C. thought. Either that, or he was trying so hard to cover up, he was coming across slow-witted.

"What's there to think about, Mr. Rudd?" Kitt asked. "Either you're positive of your statement, or you're not."

"Before I met her," he blurted out. "She had a problem. A big one."

"With what?"

"Everything. Mostly blow."

"What else did she tell you about it?"

"Not much. She was in recovery. Went to rehab."

"So you never saw her use?"

"No. Never."

"She work?"

"What?"

"Did she have a job?"

"Yeah. She didn't talk about it much."

Interesting. "Doing what?"

"Some kind of office work." He shrugged. "Filing. Shit like that."

"What about her boss? She talk about him much?"

"Never."

"Never," Kitt repeated. "Really? Said nothing at all?"

"Not that I recall," he corrected. "We had other things on our minds, if you know what I mean?"

M.C. decided he was even more of a creep than she had first thought. "Do you know of anyone who would want her dead?"

He paled. "No. No way."

"You're awfully emphatic about that."

His Adam's apple bobbed. A subtle desperation oozed from him. Like slime.

"She was a nice girl. Why would someone hurt her?"

"You tell us, Mr. Rudd."

His eyes widened. "What do you mean by that? Are you . . . you can't think I had something to do with—I couldn't . . . I wouldn't hurt her or anyone else!"

His voice rose. A couple patrons from the other end of the bar glanced their way.

Kitt stepped in, suddenly the good cop. "I'm sure my partner didn't mean to imply you were involved. Did you, Detective Riggio?"

"Of course not." She smiled. "Just curious what you might know about her death."

"Nothing! Just like I said!"

Kitt laid her card on the bar in front of him. "Call me or Detective Riggio if you think of anything else."

"Wait! What . . . what happened to her?"

M.C. stopped and looked over her shoulder, locking her gaze with his. "We're not certain yet. But we will be, Brad. Soon."

6:40 p.m.

M.C. picked up take-out Chinese food on the way to Erik's. She'd tried to call him, but he hadn't answered. If he'd eaten, they could refrigerate the Kung Pao chicken and broccoli & beef for another time. Though something told her food was the farthest thing from his mind.

She parked, climbed out, and crossed to the home's magnificent entrance. M.C. recalled the first time she had crossed this threshold, the way her jaw had dropped at first glimpse of the home's incredible interior.

That felt like a lifetime ago now.

And, oddly, it felt like yesterday as well.

She had a key, but felt funny about using it tonight and rang the bell. M.C.'s breath caught when Erik answered. He looked shattered. "Hey," she said softly and held up the take-out bags. "Chinese. I tried to call, but—"

He took the bags from her hands, set them aside and drew her into the foyer and into his arms.

And held her. As if he needed her to stay upright. As if his very breath depended on her. He bent his head, resting his cheek against her hair.

Seconds ticked past, becoming minutes. Still he held her. She felt his sadness as if it were a tangible thing. It seeped out of him, into her.

So this is what it's like to be someone's rock, she thought. *Their port in a storm.*

Their everything.

He broke the embrace. Together, silently, they carried the bags of food into the palatial great room.

He'd already opened a bottle of wine; a half-full glass sat on the coffee table.

She refused his offer of a glass and opted for water. They didn't bother with plates or forks, but passed the cartons back and forth, using the chopsticks provided by Ming's Palace.

Although Erik's skill with the sticks bordered on amazing, tonight she managed to eat more than he.

He soon gave up the pretense and went back to his wine, silently watching her eat.

After a moment, he broke the silence. "Her parents called," he said softly. Almost as if to himself.

"Suddenly concerned and attentive. They blamed me. Accused me of not doing enough for her. It was my fault."

He paused then went on, anger edging into his voice. "The same parents who had shuttled her between them, resentful of the one who didn't have her, counting the hours like a miser counting his coins. The same parents willing to simply cut her free when she turned eighteen. When all she wanted was for them to fight to keep her."

His voice cracked. It broke M.C.'s heart. For Erik. And Whitney. And for the parents for whom it was now too late.

"It's not your fault," she said.

"I feel responsible anyway."

"Relapse is part of recovery. You can't blame yourself if she—"

He cut her off. "I'm an addiction specialist. I don't need a lesson in recovery."

M.C. didn't take offense. How could she? Too many times she had done the same as he was doing now. Blamed herself for circumstances she couldn't control, rejecting every offer of comfort.

Still rejecting them, she acknowledged.

Instead, she stood. And crossed to stand before him. She held out her hand. "Come with me."

He took her hand; she led him to the bedroom. There, she drew him with her to the bed. She took his mouth in long, slow, drugging kisses, then moved on, tasting and teasing, stripping away garments, eager to feel his skin against hers. Without words, she told him how sorry she was, that she knew he hurt, that she hurt for him. Without words she allowed herself to love him.

As she took him inside her, reason evaporated. As did thoughts of lives ended too soon, of sadness or comfort. Urgency replaced them, a different kind of need. Faster, more frenzied. They crescendoed and cried out together.

Skin damp, hearts thundering, they lay twined together. M.C. trailed her mouth across his shoulder.

Erik stopped her, bringing her face to his. Looking her in the eyes.

"I love you," he murmured.

Nowhere to run. No place to hide.

She wished she could return the endearment. The *L*-word didn't slip off her lips easily. Not anymore.

Not since Dan.

So she kissed him. Deeply. Passionately.

She felt him sigh. Perhaps tonight, of all nights, he had believed he could scale the wall around her heart.

"I can only be who I am," she said, hearing the regret in her own voice.

"I know that, M.C." He rolled onto his back, bringing her with him. "I've been thinking."

"Mmhmm?" She whispered her fingers across his chest, liking the trail of goose bumps that followed.

"We could go away."

She smiled to herself. "Where would we go?"

"It doesn't matter."

"I like that. Just pick a place and go."

"Pack up and leave."

She smiled up at him. "Someplace warm, please. I'll bring a bikini."

"And I'll bring sunscreen."

She laughed lightly. "Tropical drinks. With those little umbrellas."

"As many as you want."

"I don't even remember my last vacation. And I know it wasn't nearly so wonderful."

He turned so they were face to face. "Not a holiday. Forever."

She laughed at his serious tone. "What are you talking about? We can't—"

"Yes, we can."

It began to sink in. "Run away."

"That's one way to put it. Another is, just . . . start over."

"What about my job?"

"Leave it behind. You won't need to work."

Not work? Give up being a cop? She thought of Kitt and Joe. The struggles they'd had reconciling their relationship and Kitt's badge. "What would I do?"

"Stay in bed with me."

He sounded like a little boy. Hopeful. And naughty.

She shouldn't be hurt. But she was. She shouldn't be angry. But she felt it building inside of her.

"And what about my family?"

"They could visit us," he said, obviously not hearing the edge in her voice. "And we would visit them."

He had it all figured out. And she would be along for the ride. His ride. Living off him.

"I need to work."

"No, you don't."

"Spoken like a true trust fund baby."

"I can support us. There's nothing wrong with that."

"What if I don't want that?"

"Ouch."

"It's not about the money, Erik. It's who I am."

"I know. And I love you for who you are."

"I don't think we should talk about this right now."

"Why not, M.C.?" Now he sounded angry. "Afraid I'll get too close?"

"You know why," she said softly. "You suffered a loss. Your emotions are raw. It's logical that you want to escape now, but tomorrow—"

"What about tomorrow?"

"It'll come. And it will take care of itself."

"What if I don't want that?"

She searched his expression, a chill moving over her. "I don't understand."

"What if I don't want to do this anymore? Us. This way."

"Don't say that, Erik."

"I don't know if I can."

"You're upset," she said, hearing the desperation in her voice. "Hurting. You—"

"I love you, M.C. I want you to be my wife. Marry me."

Fear, the deep cold, took her breath. "I can't," she said, choked.

"Can't, M.C.? Or won't?"

She was too broken for a relationship. No good. For him. Or anyone. "You don't understand."

"You're right," he said harshly. "I don't."

"I'll go."

She slipped out of bed, he reached up and pulled her back. "Don't go."

"You're sure?"

"Please, don't go."

He could swallow his pride for her. Make himself vulnerable. Need her.

Why couldn't she do the same?

She curled up next to him. But the way he held her was

different. Though they were nestled against each other, distant. A yawing chasm she felt to the very core of her being.

It was over. She and Erik. The feeling of dread that had come over her earlier. The premonition of an end.

She felt as if she was dying inside. But her eyes were dry. She had no more tears. She had used them all up.

Tuesday
7:20 a.m.

M.C. awakened alone. Cold, she reached for Erik's pillow and brought it to her. It smelled of him, and she breathed deeply, the scent swamping her. Memories as well. Of her and Erik's fight, her inability to commit, Dan's unnecessary death.

She hadn't slept well. Her dreams had been turbulent and disturbing—she and Dan at the altar. A gunshot. Blood spraying her white gown. But then she had been holding the gun. And it was Erik, not Dan, who lay dying at her feet. Not at a church altar, but in the woods, in the snow. The red-stained snow.

A sound passed her lips. Of despair and grief. One dredged from her very core.

She pressed her face into the pillow to stifle it.

Let it go, Mary Catherine. For the love of God, move on.

But she couldn't. M.C. balled her hands into fists. Dammit, she wanted to, but . . .

Angry at herself, she threw back the covers, climbed out of bed. The temperature had dropped dramatically overnight. She heard the wind whistling through the trees outside the bedroom windows. The clawing of branches on the glass. The cold front. The apocalyptic storm Sorenstein had been carrying-on about.

She snatched up her robe, found her slippers, and stalked to the bathroom. After relieving herself, she brushed her teeth and ran a comb through her hair.

Then went looking for Erik.

The TV in the great room was on. "Morning!" she called out, stopping in front of the seventy-inch flat-screen. The Weather Channel. A map of the U.S. showing the jet stream, the arctic air pushing all the way down to Florida, where they predicted it to collide with a tropical storm in the Atlantic before moving up the East Coast. The meteorologists were waxing ecstatic over what would happen when the two systems met.

M.C. frowned, thinking of Sorenstein's rant. "Let's just keep fucking with Mother Nature. We'll be like the dinosaurs. Extinct."

M.C. shook her head. She refused to buy into Sorenstein's doom and gloom. She couldn't. She'd been to hell and had fought her way back. To launch herself willingly into that place of despair? Never again.

She found the remote and hit the Mute button. The house went silent. Too silent. M.C. frowned and started for the kitchen.

She reached it. "Erik," she said, stepping into the room.

But he wasn't there. Not anymore, anyway. The newspaper lay open on the table, a cup of coffee beside it.

M.C. crossed to the table, glanced down at the paper. *The Register Star.* Main news, page two. A mention of Bello's death. Her picture. *Damn.* She touched the cup; it was cold.

Where was he? *His office*, she thought. *Or the music room.* Sometimes when he was upset, he lost himself in the classics.

She checked both, came up empty and headed to the garage. Sure enough, no Jeep.

Where could he have gone so early? And why hadn't he told her? Neither was like him.

Yesterday's uneasiness crept over her once more. The

memory of their argument.

"What if I don't want to do this anymore?"

And now he was gone. Without saying goodbye.

What if it was over?

She plucked her phone from the robe's deep pocket. She dialed him; her call went straight to voicemail.

He'd turned off his phone. He never turned it off. In case the clinic or a patient needed him.

He was shutting her out. Already.

It was her own fault. She deserved this.

"Hey, babe," she said. "You must have been in super-stealth mode this morning. I didn't hear you get up, dress or anything. How crazy is that?"

She sounded desperate. Panicky.

She cleared her throat, lowered her voice. "Are you okay? I just want you to know that—"

But she couldn't say what he wanted to hear. So instead, she asked him to call her and hung up.

A moment after she ended the call, another came in. She answered. "Erik?"

"It's Kitt. You sound out of breath. Are you okay?"

"I'm good. What's up?"

"Sal's called a meeting in the war room. Nine o'clock."

Salvatore Minelli, her boss, Deputy Chief of Detectives. His calling a meeting meant one of two things: somebody had fucked-up big or something had gone big-time bad.

"What's happening?" she asked, heading to dress.

"Storm preparation. This one's gonna be a monster."

9:10 a.m.

The city bigwigs were preparing for the worst-case scenario. Two feet of snow. Blizzard-force winds. The downed trees, power lines and traffic nightmares that went along with both.

Assets were being moved into the most at-risk areas. Power trucks. Plows. Once roads were impassable, it could prove impossible to get them where they were most needed for days. An emergency operations center had been set up. All sworn officers were being activated, including detectives.

"It's going to be grueling, people," Sal said. "Storm's E.T.A. is twenty-four hours from now. Make 'em count. Dismissed."

The moment M.C. exited the meeting, she tried Erik again. When it again went straight to voicemail, she tried Kids in Crisis. They hadn't heard from him but promised to have him return her call when they did.

Kitt frowned. "What's wrong?"

M.C. forced a shrug. "Nothing."

"Try that with somebody else, *partner*. Not me."

"Erik and I had a difference of opinion."

"About?"

M.C. just looked at her.

"Two days in a row? Wow, that's rough."

M.C. stiffened at the amusement in Kitt's tone. "Glad my misery could lighten your day, partner."

"Look, the man's crazy in love with you. He's a great guy, handsome and rich. You'll work this out."

"It might be over, Kitt. He said so." The words came out thick.

"You've had this discussion before."

"This time was different. He wanted me to quit—" she spread her hands, "—this. Suggested he and I just leave it all behind. Go away together."

"Do it," Kitt said simply. "Go."

M.C. couldn't believe Kitt would say that. Of all people, her partner should understand. She told her so.

"I understand, all right. I lost Joe twice. The job's not worth it."

M.C. shook her head. "I can't do it. It's not me."

"I used to say that."

"And you're still here, aren't you?" The words came out sharper than she intended. Sharper than was fair.

"Our situation was different, M.C. We lost Sadie, and I lost my focus. It's about balance. It's about knowing, to the very center of your being, what's important. With what I know now, I'd choose him. Hands down."

"He needs something I can't give him."

"Or won't?"

M.C. heard the challenge in Kitt's voice. From anyone else, even one of her brothers, she'd get her back up. The famous Riggio temper would flare. And she would push back. Hard.

But to Kitt, she owed her life.

"When it comes to love, I'm a frickin' Typhoid Mary. Every relationship. And Dan . . . I couldn't live through it." She shook her head. "Not again."

She paused, then put voice to the words that had terrified her most. "He said he didn't know if he could be with me anymore."

Kitt's expression softened with understanding. "He was in a bad place, right? Hurting. He didn't mean it."

"I think he did. The look in his eyes—and this morning, he was gone. And his phone goes straight to voicemail."

"He needs time alone. To think. To grieve. Give him some space, M.C. Erik's not the type to go off half-cocked."

M.C. opened her mouth to reply; she shut it as Kitt's cell went off. "Lundgren." She paused, obviously listening. "Interesting. Thanks."

She re-holstered the cell. "That was Frances."

"He's completed the autopsy already?"

"No. Just the initial inspection of the body. He found something he wants us to take a look at. A bruise."

"Where?"

"Middle of Bello's back."

10:30 a.m.

The morgue was located in the Public Safety Building, the same as the police department. Convenient, one-stop shopping. The autopsy room was cold. The body that had been Whitney Bello was laid out on the table. Frances' assistant stood waiting; the young man's expression far away. M.C. got that. To stay sane, you did what you had to.
Frances hadn't made the first cut. "I wanted you to see this before I went any further."

"You're thinking it's a game-changer?"

"Maybe."

Frances Roselli was a cautious man. Meticulous. A maybe from him spoke volumes.

He motioned his assistant. They tipped up the body. There it was, a crescent-shaped bruise in the middle of her back. An ugly purple, it stood out in bold contrast to the ghostly white of the skin around it.

Kitt looked at M.C. "What could have caused this?"

M.C. bent for a better look. Dark. Almost black. The outline clear. She frowned. It would have taken a vicious blow or intense, localized pressure.

She looked at Frances. "No other scratches or bruises?"

"Nothing other than what we discussed at the scene."

"You have a theory?"

"I do, indeed, Detectives. If you'll indulge me, I have a prop."

Frances retrieved a plastic bag. Inside was a man's shoe. Thick sole, sturdy heel.

"Imagine our Ms. Bello, face-down, partially in the water. How she ended up in that position, we don't know. But I believe she wasn't alone. I believe her companion placed his foot here—"

He illustrated with the shoe. The outside edge of the heel mirrored the crescent shape of the bruise.

"Son of a bitch," M.C. said.

"The fact the bruise is localized and darker along the outside edge," Frances went on, "makes sense."

Kitt agreed. "The riverbank sloped down. His weight was on his heel, so he didn't fall in himself."

"Which explains her hands," M.C. said. "She fought, tried to claw her way out."

"Exactly." Frances and his assistant repositioned the body on the table. "Is it enough to classify her death a homicide? No. But it's enough to raise doubts this was an accident."

M.C. thought of Erik. "Which means drugs may or may not have been part of the equation. I want that tox report now."

"Two weeks, Detective. You know the drill. But autopsy will offer us more information. Give me a couple hours with her, I'll see what I can uncover."

The moment they exited the morgue, M.C. dialed Erik. As before, she got his voicemail. "Call me back," she said. "I have news about Whitney."

She hung up to find Kitt watching her. "It's going to be okay."

"Is it?"

Kitt grinned. "Want to take out your nerves on someone deserving?"

"Bello's boyfriend?"

"You're reading my mind, partner. That prick was holding back. Let's exert some pressure."

M.C. offered to drive, and as they eased out of the parking garage, M.C.'s cell went off. She hit the hands-free. "Riggio."

"This is Sanchez, from communications. We just got a call-in from a Parks and Recreation employee. Vehicle abandoned in Anna Page Park, engine running."

"We're Violent Crimes, Sanchez. Try Field Services."

"Lieutenant Bell said to call you first, that you'd want this."

She and Bell had worked together before he'd been promoted to head of communications. M.C. frowned. "He say why, Sanchez?"

"Negative, Detective. Just wanted me to tell you the vehicle's registered to one Erik Sundstrand, National Avenue, Rockford."

10:50 a.m.

The sight of Erik's jeep, driver's-side door open, engine running, nearly brought her to her knees. M.C. slammed out of her Explorer and crossed to the responding officer.

"Detective Riggio," she barked out, stopping directly in front of him. "Talk to me."

He was young and looked nervous at having a detective in his face that way. He shifted his gaze from her to Kitt, then back. "Got the call from the park ranger. Came in about two hours ago. Found the vehicle open and running. He called out, searched the immediate area, checked the closest restrooms. No sign of the vehicle's owner."

"Have you touched anything?"

"Negative. Took a visual survey of the interior and surrounding vicinity."

A moment later she and Kitt stood beside the Jeep.

Kitt looked at her. "Can you do this?"

Her heart was beating so hard she thought it might burst out of her chest. "Yes," she said evenly. "I'm fine. Absolutely."

"Then prove it. Keep your shit together."

They searched the Jeep. Nothing to suggest any kind of struggle or violence. Nothing personal had been left behind—no wallet, cell phone, not even a pack of gum. Erik disliked feeling constricted while driving and almost always removed his coat, either tossing it in back or laying it across the passenger seat. Its absence suggested he'd slipped it on, then climbed out of the car. As if to greet someone.

Then he'd disappeared.

Who could he have been meeting? And why here?

"Let's get Sorenstein and company out here," Kitt said. "They can process the scene."

"Let's just leave. Go away."

Maybe he had done that? Made a fresh start.

Without her.

No, that was crazy. She realized her hands were shaking and stuffed them into her pockets. That was just talk. A man like Erik, one with so many responsibilities, didn't do that. Couldn't do that.

"M.C." Kitt said, interrupting her thoughts. "You said Erik was upset last night."

"Yes."

"Despondent?"

"I guess. Bello's parents called, they blamed him. He took it hard."

"And then you argued? Over your relationship? He asked you to marry him again."

"Yes. But—"

"How despondent was he, M.C.?"

She realized what Kitt was intimating and shook her head. "No. There's no way he would . . . no."

"Kill himself? Are you sure of that?"

He'd felt he failed Whitney. Had said he didn't think he could go on the way they had been.

And she hadn't even thrown him a scrap.

"I'm positive," she said, though she didn't like any of the possibilities running through her head. They all took her somewhere she didn't want to go.

"There are other options, M.C. Erik's a powerful and wealthy man. A target for those who might want to profit from hurting him."

One of those places. God, no. Not yet. "Maybe he's hurt. He likes to run. Especially when he needs to work things out. Maybe he fell. Broke his leg or—"

"If he went for a run, why leave his vehicle running?"

It didn't make sense. She knew it, but wasn't ready to fully face it.

"I grew up on this side of town. I know this park. There's a trail along a—"

A large retention pond. Not two hundred yards away. Over the hill.

Whitney Bello had drowned.

"How despondent was he, M.C.?"

M.C. reacted to the thought and ran for the hill. Kitt called after her, but she didn't stop until she topped the hill. The pond, its surface as smooth as glass, mocked her.

What did you hope to see, Mary Catherine?

She brought the heels of her hands to her eyes. She had to slow down, get a grip.

Do it, Mary Catherine. Focus.

She reached the edge of the pond, scanned the perimeter. Nothing. She started around it, eyes darting back and forth. The sun broke out from behind a cloud. Something winked at her from the weeds.

She went to it. An iPhone 5. Or what was left of one. It'd been smashed. Or stomped. And tossed.

Erik had an iPhone 5.

She sank to her knees. Kitt came up beside her. "You don't know that it's his."

M.C. agreed, though that was a lie. In her heart, she knew. The premonition. Her dread.

"I called in Canataldi and Baker."

M.C. looked up at her and frowned. "Why? We've got this."

"I'm handing it over, M.C. It's the smart thing to do."

"That's bullshit." She got to her feet. "I'm okay. My shit's together."

"It's not, M.C. You're not. Besides, we're working Bello."

"We'll hand her to them. This is Erik, for God's sake! I'm not—"

Kitt caught her hands, looked her dead in the eyes. "Let it go. It's done."

Furious, she freed her hands and stalked back to the scene. Canataldi and Baker had arrived. Neither of them looked her directly in the eyes.

Typhoid Mary. Get involved with Mary Catherine Riggio, and it ended badly for you. Always.

She marched up to them. "You tell me you've got this. Look me in the eyes and tell me that. No fucking up."

"We've got this, Riggio," Baker said. "I promise you."

Canataldi concurred. "For you, Riggio. We'll locate him."

"I found a smashed iPhone near the pond. It could be Erik's." She cleared her throat. "We need to know the last call he made and received. The cell tower pings."

"We'll take care of it."

This was Erik. How did she let go?

"I want to know everything," she said. "Every step of the way."

"Absolutely."

"I'll be on you like white on frickin' rice. Don't even contemplate slacking off or giving up, because I'll kick your—"

"We won't." Baker laid a hand on her shoulder, gave it a gentle squeeze. "You have my word."

2:25 p.m.

The next several hours were a nightmare. Baker and Canataldi questioned her, then questioned her again. Personal questions. About her and Erik's relationship, the events of the night before and about his state of mind.

As of this moment, no one had heard from him. Every possible contact had been called, from the various divisions of his company, SunCorp, to the members of the many boards he sat on. His personal calendar had been clear for this morning. Warrant to access mobile phone tracks had been given and delivered to Erik's carrier.

The weather had begun to turn. The wind had kicked up, the sky turning an ominous slate gray.

The squad room went silent as M.C. entered. Suddenly everybody was too busy to even look up.

News travelled fast in the ranks; bad news travelled faster.

Kitt touched her arm. "I need to bring Sal up to speed. You'll be okay."

It wasn't a question but an affirmation. M.C. smiled grimly. "Thanks."

"Detective Riggio?"

She looked over her shoulder at Nan, the unit secretary.

"Messages?"

"Your pizza."

"I didn't order a pizza."

"It came for you an hour and a half ago. A Mama Riggio's. Maybe your brothers sent it?"

Her three youngest brothers, Tony, Max and Frank, did that sometimes. Sent over a pie when the restaurant was slow or they knew she was in the middle of an intense investigation and needed nourishment.

"I was afraid to leave it on your desk or in the lunch room. Figured it'd be gone before you got back."

"Thanks, Nan." She retrieved the pie.

"Detective Riggio?" M.C. looked back. The woman's face puckered with concern. "I heard about . . . your friend and . . . I hope everything turns out okay."

A lump formed in her throat. Unable to speak, she just nodded then walked away.

The lunchroom was deserted. Usually just the thought of one of her brothers' pies had her mouth watering. Today, nothing. Though she had no desire to eat, her body needed the fuel.

She flipped open the box. And caught her breath. A smiley face. Made out of pepperoni.

It grinned up at her, mocking. Somehow sinister. *Gotcha!* it seemed to say. *Joke's on you!*

Her brothers didn't mean it that way. Even if they were three sadistic sons-of-bitches who hated her guts, they didn't know about Erik. Sal had put a gag order on the case. Erik was an important man in Rockford, from an important family. His disappearance would be big news. But the timing was like a kick in the gut anyway.

She stared at it, a sick feeling forming in the pit of her stomach. She opened her phone and dialed Mama Riggio's. The hostess answered. "Hey Judy. One of my ass kissing brothers around?"

"They're in a meeting. And judging by the volume of their

discussion, interrupting would be a very bad idea."

They did that. Loved each other to death and wanted to kill each other at the same time.

"Just wanted to thank them for the pizza they sent over this afternoon."

"Wasn't that cute?"

Not quite how she'd describe it.

"Adorable," she said.

"But it wasn't from them."

"I'm sorry, what?"

"They didn't order it."

A chill moved over her. "Who did, Judy?"

"It was a phone order. He said he was a friend of yours and wanted to brighten your day. Hold on—"

M.C. heard her shuffling through the order book.

"Here it is. Mr. Foo Beech."

M.C. frowned. "Foo Beech? Could you spell that?"

"Sure. F-U-"Judy stopped, obviously realizing Mr. Beech had been sending M.C. more than a pizza.

Fuck you, bitch.

It was happening again.

M.C.'s knees buckled. She sat hard, thoughts racing.

"God, I'm so sorry . . . It was a phone order—"

Someone wanted to hurt her. They were doing it through Erik.

"I never would have—"

Her fault. He was in danger, maybe dead. Because of her.

Kitt entered the break room. "I heard you had a Mama Riggio's— " She stopped short. "What happened?"

M.C. motioned to the pizza box.

"—believe me, M.C., I never—"

She cut her off. "It's okay, Judy. I know you wouldn't." From the corners of her eyes, she saw Kitt lift the box's lid, heard her soft exhalation of breath.

M.C. refocused on Judy. "How did he pay for the pie? Credit card?"

"He would have had to . . ." She sounded rattled. "I can't think. I—"

"It's okay, take all the time you need."

"Hold on, let me check." It took only a moment. "No, a gift card."

"Do you keep a record of who purchases the cards?"

"No. Besides, it wasn't one of ours. One of those pre-paid VISA gift cards."

Outmaneuvered. Dammit!

"Thanks, Judy. Look, do me a favor. Don't bother my brothers with this right now. It's nothing, okay? And you know how they get."

Judy did know. She had five brothers, and their protective streaks ran a mile wide. Never mind that she carried a gun and could take down a man twice her size, nobody messed with *their* sister.

M.C. ended the call and looked at Kitt. "Whoever took Erik did it to punish me."

"You got all that from a smiley-face pizza?"

"Yeah. Sent to me compliments of Mr. F-U-Beech." She gave Kitt a moment to process, then went on.

"A phone order, paid for with a gift card."

"Which they keep no records of."

"Exactly."

"You don't know for certain—"

"A couple hours after Erik disappears, I receive this with the message *Fuck you, bitch*. What do you think?"

"Someone you busted. Testified against."

She nodded. "Someone with an ax to grind. Recently released or paroled."

"Who comes to mind?" Kitt asked.

"Frickin' everyone."

"Okay, let's slow this down. Mama Riggio's have caller ID?"

"I don't know."

"You find out. If they don't, we get the number through

the carrier. I'm sure Mama Riggio's will have a record of the exact time that order came in. In the meantime, I'll bring Baker and Canataldi up to speed."

M.C. was already dialing. "I'll access the database, see if any of my angry scumbags have hit the street recently."

6:10 p.m.

Mama Riggio's did, indeed, have caller ID. In addition, their system logged the number of every phone order.

The smiley-face pizza's phone number belonged to a nasty piece of work named Dickey Larson. An all-around dirtbag. In and out of jail all his life. Drug abuser, wife beater, cheat ,and thief. Last go-around, M.C. had convinced his wife to testify against him, then loaned her the money to relocate. Dickey hadn't made a secret of being mightily pissed off.

A few minutes ago they'd hauled his ass in for questioning; Baker had handed M.C. the honor, and she was chomping at the bit to get started.

She faced the slimy little worm across the interview table. "You like pizza, Dickey?"

He smirked. "It's all right."

"You like Mama Riggio's?"

He shrugged. "Sure. Who doesn't?"

"How about me, Dickey. How do you feel about me?"

He couldn't hide the hatred burning in his eyes. She could feel the animosity radiating off him in waves. "No feelings at all."

"At your trial you called me a bitch. You said you'd make me pay."

"I wasn't thinking straight."

"Isn't it true that you blame me for your wife leaving you?"

"Good riddance."

"You ever hear the name Erik Sundstrand?"

"Nah."

Not even a blink. "You sure? Sundstrand's a pretty recognizable name around here."

"I've heard the name *Sundstrand* before. But I don't know that dude."

"You order a pizza today?"

"I don't know what you're talking about."

"Really?" She flipped up the lid. "This pizza?"

Another smirk. Turd couldn't help himself. "Since when did ordering a pizza become a crime?"

"So you did?"

"Whatever."

"Not whatever, Mr. *Beech*. Why did you send me this?"

"Who's Mr. Beech? I don't know nobody by that name."

She cocked her head. "You're not very smart, are you?"

That pissed him off. She saw it and smiled. "That's why you keep getting caught. Stupid."

His face flamed red. "Shut up."

"Just a big, stupid loser. Isn't that right, Dickey? You're just a—"

"Fuck you, bitch!"

She nodded and sat back in her chair. "Now that's exactly what I'm talking about. That's a threat. Sending the cop who busted you that message is not how you stay out of trouble."

There was no trace of the smirk now. "It's a happy face. It was supposed to make you smile."

"And the *Fuck you, bitch*. Was that supposed to make me smile, too?"

He didn't respond, and she went on. "You know what else is stupid? Kidnapping somebody. Really stupid."

"What does that have to do with me? Nuthin'."

"Aggravated kidnapping carries up to a thirty-year sentence. For a repeat offender like you, the maximum would definitely be in order."

"What the hell are you talking about?"

"I convinced your wife to press charges against your ugly ass."

"And I did my time. Every damned day of it!"

"What did you think about while you were in? About your wife? The fact that I convinced her to press charges? That she testified against you?"

He didn't reply and she went on. "You promised you'd hurt me. That you'd make me pay."

"It's a fucking pizza! What's the big deal?"

"You told me—" she read what he'd shouted after the verdict, as they led him away. "Wait, bitch. Just wait. I'm going to make you pay." She lifted her gaze to his. "Isn't that what you said?"

"I was pissed off. What would you have said?"

"I'm more interested in your actions. You wanted to hurt me. You blamed me for your wife leaving."

"The heat of the moment."

"Where were you this morning?"

"Home."

"Alone?"

"My wife left me. Remember?"

"Did you arrange a meeting with Erik Sundstrand?"

"I told you, I don't know the dude!"

"You lured him out to Anna Page Park? And once he was there, you abducted him."

"Holy shit!" He jumped to his feet. "No. No way! I sent you a pizza. That's all. I wanted to mess with you, that's all! I swear to God! And I want my fucking lawyer!"

"M.C.? Kitt?"

Baker. He motioned them out to the hallway. "Got Sundstrand's phone tracks. The last number he received doesn't match Larson's."

7:15 p.m.

"It doesn't mean anything, Kitt," M.C. said, minutes later. They stood in the observation room, watching as Larson alternately paced and sat slumped in the chair, head in his hands. Baker and Canataldi had gone for a burger while they waited for the Public Defender. "He used a pre-paid, throwaway cell phone to contact Erik. So there wouldn't be a trail."

"So why didn't he use it to order the pizza?"

"Because he's a dumb shit."

"Exactly. He's not a thinker, M.C. He's a bully. I don't think he's your guy. This is too big for him."

M.C. shook her head in denial of Kitt's words. "He's the one. He has to be."

"I'm sorry."

"The pizza, the same day Erik disappears? C'mon, Kitt, it's too much of a coincidence."

"Coincidences happen. They do, M.C."

"Not this time." She curved her hands into fists. "What about his threat to make me pay?"

"How many times have perps threatened you?"

Too many to count. "He has Erik." She heard the

desperation in her voice; she knew Kitt must also.

"Maybe you're right. This pizza stunt violates his parole, so he's not going anywhere. It gives us time."

"But what about Erik's time? How much does he have?"

"Detectives?" Nan stuck her head in the door. "Public Defender's arrived."

M.C. started for the door; Kitt stopped her. "The team's decided you should observe this time."

She opened her mouth to protest. Try reasoning with Kitt, beg if she had to. *The effort would be wasted,* M.C. acknowledged. This time the decision was bigger than her partner.

"You've got to break him, Kitt. If he knows where Erik is—"

"We'll find out." Kitt squeezed her hand. "I promise."

M.C. couldn't sit. She paced. Waiting for them to begin. Feeling the clock ticking. Bringing the storm closer. Putting more distance between her and Erik.

The players assembled in the interview room. Exchanged greetings. *Screw the pleasantries,* she wanted to scream. *Make the bastard talk. Anything. Do anything.*

At her hip, her cell phone vibrated. "Detective Riggio," she answered, gaze on the video monitor.

"Mary Catherine Riggio?" the man asked.

The hair on the back of her neck prickled. He had her full attention now. "Yes?"

"Bill McCormack. SunCorp, COO. Erik introduced us at the Christmas party."

The image of the man—short and balding, Harry Potter glasses, a sharp gaze that missed nothing—popped into her head. His voice sounded strange.

"Of course," she said. "I assume you're calling for an update but unfortunately, I have nothing to report."

"It's not—" He cleared his throat. "I do. Have something to report."

His voice shook badly. She grabbed the back of the chair

for support, waiting for the rest. And for the moment her world crumbled beneath her feet.

"A Fed-Ex envelope," he continued. "Waiting on my doorstep, when I got home tonight. In it was—"

He choked back what sounded like a sob. "Erik's driver's license. And a bloody paper towel."

8:25 p.m.

Despite the wind and blowing snow, M.C. made it to McCormack's east side home in record time. She had simply reacted. Left HQ without a word to anyone. She'd rather have Kitt with her, but had feared the team would shut her out.

He was waiting and opened the door the moment she reached it. She stepped quickly inside, snapping it shut behind her.

"Where are they?" she asked.

He led her to the kitchen. He had laid the three items—envelope, license and paper towel—on the kitchen counter. She gazed at them, a metallic taste in her mouth. Fear. Deep and ice cold.

Her voice, however, was steady when she asked, "How much did you handle them?"

"I didn't know I shouldn't," he said, tone anguished. "The envelope was propped by the door . . . it'd been a long, upsetting day. I've been, we've all been so worried—I grabbed it on my way inside, then opened it."

He swallowed hard. "It wasn't until I pulled out the . . . contents that I took a closer look at the envelope and saw—"

"That it didn't have a shipping label."

He nodded. "I didn't know what else to do, so I called

you."

"You did the right thing."

"What does it mean?"

She had a pretty good idea. One she couldn't voice yet. She needed to steady herself first, slow her heart, tamp back the panic. McCormack's house phone rang. He looked at her, fear racing into his eyes.

"You need to get that," she said softly.

He shook his head. It rang again.

She crossed to the device, noticed it had a speaker option. Time would run out. It always did.

It rang again. M.C. snatched up the device, handed it to him then pressed the Speaker button.

"Hello," he answered, voice sounding strangled.

"Mr. McCormack?"

"Yes?"

"I see you got your delivery."

"Where's Erik?"

M.C. closed her eyes in an attempt to listen with all her senses. To pick up something, in the man's voice or from the background noise, that would lead to her to Erik.

"That's a stupid question, McCormack. The smart question is, how do you get him back?"

"How do I get him back?"

"Seven hundred-fifty thousand dollars. Cash. Tomorrow at noon."

"But I can't get—"

"Yes, you can. And you will. Or Mr. Sundstrand dies."

"Wait! Where do I—"

"Instructions will come. And, Mr. McCormack? No police. That would be very dangerous for Sundstrand."

10:50 p.m.

For the first time, M.C. truly understood the "no cops" dilemma. Before, she'd been arrogant. Law enforcement was essential. The only way to catch the perp and save the victim. Heeding the kidnapper's demands was, frankly, stupid. And an almost certain death sentence for the victim. When it was someone you cared about, that arrogance became gut-wrenching fear. Of making a misstep. Causing a worst-case-scenario.

Faced with the threat of harm to Erik, she'd hesitated. Her, a cop. She had even considered taking on the kidnappers by herself. Wiring the phone, making the drop, all of it. Dangerous thoughts. More arrogance.

So she had made the call. The team had arrived at McCormack's moments ago.

"Seven hundred-fifty grand," Kitt was saying. "Why that amount? Sundstrand's worth millions."

"Small-time hoods," Baker offered. "Not so bright."

"Or very bright," McCormack said.

They all looked at him.

"I can write a check for up to that amount, my signature only. Anything more requires Erik's as well."

The group went silent. Kitt broke it first. "Not a guess

then. They knew."

"Someone on the inside."

"Ex-employee? Family member maybe?"

M.C. looked at McCormack. "Who else has access to that information?"

"Any number of people. From department heads to our bank rep."

M.C. jumped to her feet. "Dammit!"

"We've got another problem," McCormack said. "A local bank doesn't keep that kind of cash on hand. It's going to have to come from a Federal Reserve Bank."

"You've got to be kidding me?"

"I wish I was, Detective."

"I'd bet my right nut that's something they didn't know." Canataldi looked at McCormack. "Where's the nearest Federal Reserve?"

"Beloit."

"Wisconsin?" M.C. sat back down. "They're ankle-deep in snow already."

"And the bank doesn't even open until nine."

"If it opens at all. We're all gonna be ass-deep in this blizzard by then."

The end of the world, Sorenstein had said. Her world.

"I'll go," M.C. said. "Arrange the drop, I'll—"

"You'll what? Break into the Federal Reserve Bank?" Kitt signaled Baker. "Time to call in the Bureau."

Wednesday
6:10 a.m.

M.C. sat at her desk. She held onto her emotions as tightly as she could. At any minute, she could lose that grip. And spin out of her freaking mind. Totally lose it.

Progress had slowed to a crawl. The Feds had taken over, shut them out. Shut her out. Luckily, Kitt and Baker were still on scene; information trickled through.

The Feds had been able to make things happen, although the timing was going to be tricky.

Arrangements with the bank had been made, the highway department would assure the armored truck's safe arrival at McCormack's. The local suits would take it from there. Marked bills. Tracking device on the package. The agent making the drop. Snipers in place. All made nearly impossible by the blizzard.

The storm was the true wild card in this one.

She'd been unable to get the location of the drop out of Kitt. She understood both the need for secrecy and her partner's position. But that didn't mean she liked or accepted it.

Sal arrived. He nodded in her direction, then retreated to his office. Everybody was hunkering down.

Waiting for the emergency calls to start flowing.

While the suits had been busy worrying about the money, the drop and making certain the perp was apprehended, she'd worried about Erik. Where he was. Whether he was protected from the elements, alive or dead. Or near death. Waiting for her to come.

Because he believed in her. Her abilities.

And in her feelings for him. Even when she didn't believe in them herself.

"Good morning, Detective. Ready for our snow-pocalypse?"

She looked blankly up at the pathologist. "Frances?"

"Last time I checked."

She didn't smile and he cocked an eyebrow. "I have my report on Whitney Bello."

That penetrated. "And?"

"Water in her lungs. Dirt and other organisms as well. Still waiting on toxicology." He handed her a file. "I thought you'd appreciate a hard copy. Didn't expect to find you here."

"Thank you." She stared at it a moment, then back up at him. "What's your excuse for the hour? Chief put you on call?"

He laughed and shook his head. "Knocking a few out before the world comes to a screeching halt. Hope to God I haven't stayed too long."

"Better get out of here, then. If you get in trouble, call me. My cousin owns a plow service."

He thanked her, then turned to leave. After a couple of steps, he looked back. "I've got a feeling about this one."

She frowned. "The storm?"

"No. About Bello. This case. There's more to it."

The image of the crescent-shaped bruise popped into her head. "Something come up during—"

"Autopsy?" He shook his head. "Nothing but the fact she was a healthy young woman with her whole life ahead of her."

After he'd left, M.C. lowered her gaze to the autopsy

report. *A healthy young woman, her whole life ahead of her.*

Where there was smoke, there was fire. If it walked like a duck and quacked like a duck, it was a duck. All those old clichés were clichés for a reason. They were almost always true.

Exactly why she had been certain Dickey Larson had been their guy. He'd been eliminated as a suspect when the ransom call had come while he'd been in custody. He could have an accomplice, but none of them thought so. Even her.

Unable to sit still, she jumped to her feet. Thoughts racing, she began to pace. Bello turns up dead. Bello worked for Erik. A day later Erik's kidnapped.

A coincidence? Or smoke?

M.C.'s thoughts turned to the boyfriend. Bradley Rudd. He'd lied. About Bello never talking about her boss. Pretending he couldn't remember the name of the place she worked. Those evasions and untruths hadn't seemed important at the time.

She went still. They did now.

Why would he lie about something ostensibly so inconsequential? To distance himself from Kids in Crisis. From Erik. Of course.

The son of a bitch had been under their noses all along.

7:45 a.m.

Bradley Rudd lived in a small brick home on Latham. One story. Eight hundred square feet, if she was being generous. There were a lot of houses like this one on the west side. She should know, she'd grown up not that far from here.

She rang the bell, then pounded. After several minutes of that, Rudd answered. He looked like someone had used his face as a punching bag. Two black eyes. Split lip. Swollen jaw.

"Detective Riggio," she said. "You remember me, don't you?"

"Go away." Before he could slam on her, she had her gun out and in his face. "We either talk here or downtown. Your choice."

"I don't know what happened to Whitney—"

"But I think you do."

"Go to hell."

She was already there. "What happened? Did she catch on? Realize you were pumping her for information? Is that why you killed her?"

"I'm calling the cops. This is harass—"

"Call 'em, stud. You think anybody's coming out in this shit? It's just you, me, and my friend, Mr. Glock."

Fear raced into his eyes. He stepped back from the door

and she slipped inside. Suitcases, she saw.

Packed and ready.

"Going somewhere?"

"Vacation."

"Tell me about Erik Sundstrand."

"I don't know what you're talking about."

Her control slipped a fraction. "Game's over, Rudd. You used Whitney to obtain information about Sundstrand. She either caught on to you or simply ceased being useful, so you killed her."

"You're crazy! I don't know—"

She totally lost it. She charged him, knocking him backward. In a flash she was on top of him, gun's barrel pressed to his battered temple. "You tell me the fucking truth, or I'll blow your fucking head off!"

He crumbled. Started shaking and crying. "I didn't do it. I swear, I didn't . . . I liked Whitney . . . it was his idea. I introduced her to him and when he found out she worked for Sundstrand—"

"Who?" She pressed the gun tighter. "Who is he?"

"My step-brother, Chuck. He hates Sunndstrand. After Wet 'n Wild closed down, he worked for SunCorp. Only a few months. Sundstrand fired him."

Rudd was blubbering now. "All I had to do was try to get some information from her. Pretend to be super-interested in her job. Ask questions."

"Why'd he kill her?"

"She caught me going through her purse. Looking for her SunCorp I.D."

"Then what?"

"She flipped out. Broke up with me."

"But you said you talked to her Sunday?"

"Chuck did. Not me. Arranged a meeting—"

"Why would she meet him at the river?"

"He's my brother. He told her he wanted to talk to her about me."

And she'd agreed. Women could be so stupid when it came to men.

"I didn't know," he whispered. "He told me he would patch things up between her and . . . I didn't know," he said again. "Until you and your partner came into Spanky's. Then I confronted him."

His voice cracked. "He laughed at me. Called me a pussy and told me if I said anything to anyone, he'd kill me."

"But you're talking now."

"I'm not that guy! I'm not . . . like him. He's got Sundstrand. Not me."

"Where does he have him stashed?"

"I don't know."

She pressed on the barrel. "Bullshit!"

He was sobbing now. "I don't, I swear!"

"Last name?"

"What? I don't—"

"Chuck's last name! What is it?"

"Same as mine. Rudd."

7:45 a.m.

M.C. dialed Kitt from the Explorer. "I've got the kidnapper's name," she said. "Chuck Rudd."

"Rudd? Wasn't that—"

"Bello's boyfriend's name? Yeah. It's his step-brother. He killed Bello when she caught on to them. Brad Rudd swears he doesn't know where Erik is. Says his involvement started and stopped with Bello. The step-brother lives with his old man." She rattled off the address. "Go get him. Find out where Erik is."

"Wait! Where's the boyfriend?"

"Handcuffed to a support in his basement. Waiting for you to pick him up."

"What are you doing now?"

"Acting on a hunch."

7:55 a.m.

The first of the snow had hit the ground and melted. That had been hours ago. Now, M.C. faced a white nightmare. The snow fell so heavily, she couldn't see five feet in front of her, let alone drive across town.

She had an idea where Erik was. And if she was right, he was exposed to the elements.

After Wet 'n Wild closed down, he went to work for Sundstrand.

Wet 'n Wild. A water park. Unable to compete with the Parks and Recreation Department's bigger Magic Waters, it'd gone belly-up. She'd driven by the abandoned park just the other day, its water slides like hulking skeletons against the gray sky.

The perfect place to stash a kidnap victim.

Or hide a body.

No. Erik was alive. And every minute counted.

She peered through the windshield, the wipers struggling to keep up. She couldn't chance doing this on her own and ending up in a ditch. Time to call in the reinforcements.

She dialed her cousin, Nikki. "Nik, it's M.C."

"Mary Catherine? This is a—"

"Is Vinnie home?"

"Vinnie? Lord, no. This blizzard's an early boon for business. He's been out plowing and salting all night."

"I need to reach him, Nik. It's an emergency."

8:25 a.m.

Vinnie had come for her, few questions asked. When family called, you answered. It was as simple as that. When the huge dump truck had rolled to a stop in front of her house, she'd darted out, looking like a baby blue abominable snowman. Snowmobile bib and jacket, boots, Glock nestled securely in her shoulder holster, extra magazine in the jacket's zipper pocket. And when she'd directed him to the abandoned water park out on Old Trask Bridge Road, he'd said nothing, just hunkered down in his seat and tightened his grip on the wheel.

She was operating on instinct and adrenaline. By focusing on the next moment, her next step. She forced everything else, all the what-ifs, out of her mind.

Even in the heavy truck, the industrial-grade plow blade clearing their way, their progress was slow.

And as the roads became more rural, their progress became tortoise-like. It was all she could do to keep from screaming in frustration.

Vinnie carried emergency gear: thermal blankets, camping heater, emergency radio, food and water. Even plows got stuck sometimes.

Not this time. She balled her hands into tight fists. Not

until she found Erik.

"You want to talk about it?"

M.C. glanced at him. He resembled her brothers and a lot of the guys she'd grown up with. Dark hair and eyes, olive-toned skin, the same macho swag. And the same big heart.

"No."

He ignored her. "This Sundstrand guy, he somebody special to you?"

A simple question. One that could be answered just as simply. Yes. Or no. But suddenly, simple wasn't an option. It was complicated. Very.

She tried to tell him so; her throat closed over the words. Her eyes burned. She blinked against the tears. She would not cry. She had promised herself. *Adapt or die.* Just like Sorenstein had said.

But now, all that didn't matter.

They had arrived.

8:55 a.m.

"This doesn't look promising," Vinnie said, peering out the windshield between wiper swipes.

It didn't. No other plow had been anywhere near the park. A winter wonderland of undisturbed, fresh snow.

If there had been human activity out here, it'd been before the snow began to fall.

They sat outside the main gate. It was secured with a heavy chain and padlock. She stared at it, stomach sinking as she realized she hadn't thought to bring a bolt cutter. She shifted her gaze. Ten-foot fencing topped with barbed wire circled the park. Mountainous snowdrifts obscuring whole sections.

She looked at Vinnie. "Can you take it down?"

Vinnie hesitated only a moment. "You bet your ass." He raised the plow blade to eye level, then shifted into reverse. The truck rumbled back, then he stopped, met her eyes. "Seat belt."

M.C. fastened hers and held on. He shoved the truck into gear and hit the gas. Even with the harness, her head snapped forward on impact with the fence. The screech of shredding metal filled her ears. The groan and pop of snapping wires. The truck shuddered to a stop.

M.C. didn't wait to confer with Vinnie. She unfastened her belt and launched out of the cab. The snow was thigh-deep in parts. Heavy and wet. She slogged through it, heading to the center of the park and its only substantial building. She'd visited Wet 'n Wild once with her nephew. He'd fallen and cut open his chin. The infirmary had been cool inside; she remembered being grateful for the air conditioning.

She heard Vinnie behind her. He called her name. She glanced back, saw that he carried blanket and first aid kit. Bless the man. She'd owe him big for this one.

M.C. motioned him to follow, then pressed on. When she reached the cinderblock structure, she was sweating. Another padlock, she saw. This one easily handled with two shots.

"Erik!" she shouted, stepping inside, weapon out. *A welcome area and sales office*, she remembered.

Empty now. She swung right. A short hallway. The infirmary had been at the end, restrooms between.

"Erik!" she called again, the silence terrifying. "Where are you?"

A shuffling sound came from the men's room. She bit back a cry, forcing herself to go slow, exercise caution. Anyone could be behind that door.

She eased it open. Erik. Wrapped in a bloodied blanket. Blindfolded and gagged. Chained to one of the stalls.

But alive.

The cry of relief spilled from her lips. She ran to him, knelt down and went to work on the gag and blindfold. "It's okay," she whispered over and over, like a mantra. "You're okay. It's going to be fine."

The gag came off first, then the blindfold. She realized her cheeks were wet, that Vinnie was standing in the doorway and that Erik needed medical attention. The timing couldn't be worse, but she didn't give a damn.

She gently cupped his face in her palms. "Yes," she said, looking him dead in the eyes. "I love you. And yes, I will marry you."

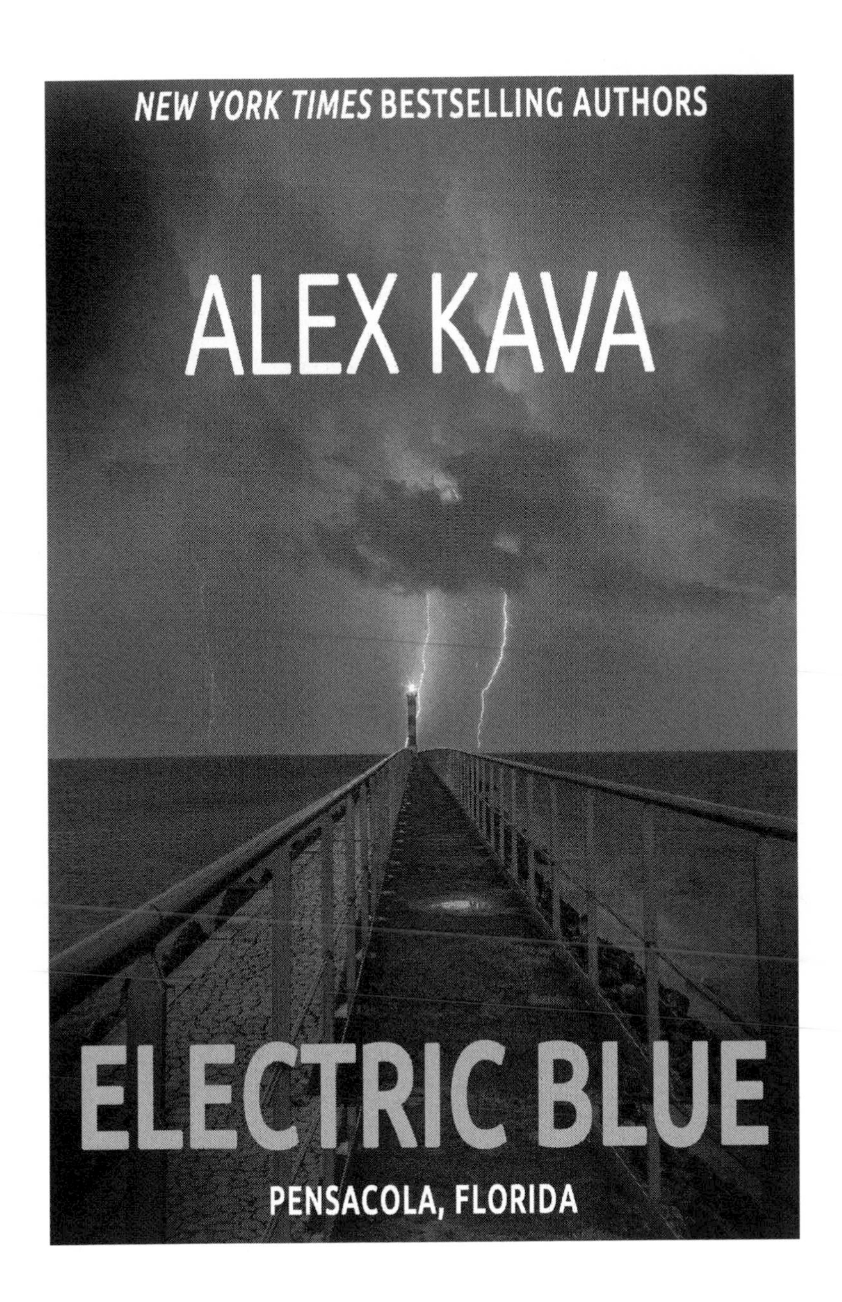
NEW YORK TIMES BESTSELLING AUTHORS
ALEX KAVA
ELECTRIC BLUE
PENSACOLA, FLORIDA

Chapter 1

Gulf of Mexico
Pensacola, Florida

FBI AGENT MAGGIE O'DELL STARED at the helicopter. She stood so close she could feel the vibration of the engine even as it idled. The soft, slow whir of the blades already made her nauseated though she could barely hear them with the gusts of wind. She watched the crew methodically run through the last of their flight checks and she still couldn't believe she had agreed to this.

It had been a year since her last excursion and she had promised herself never ever again to set foot inside another helicopter. Yet here she was. All decked out in a flight suit. It was red-orange, what she knew the Coasties affectionately called "mustangs." The suits were designed to provide flotation and were also fire retardant. Neither of which added much comfort to Maggie. This time her suit was complete with a helmet with ICS (internal communication system). The ICS was a step up. Last time they didn't let her communicate with them.

She glanced over at her partner, R.J. Tully. He stood back about a hundred feet from the helipad where he'd be safe and sound from the downwash when they lifted off. He gave her a forced grin and a thumbs-up. Maggie still felt like she had gotten the short straw, though of course, they hadn't drawn straws. They were professionals. Although standing here with cockroaches gnawing inside her stomach she might offer Tully rock/paper/scissors or a toss of a coin and not care how childish it sounded. But she had been up with this aircrew before. Somehow that made her win—or lose—depending on one's perspective.

She needed to block out how the clouds had turned day into dusk though it was barely noon. *Was that a raindrop she felt?* How much longer before the sky burst open? She needed to stay focused and concentrate on the reason she and Tully were here.

A United States senator's family was missing—somewhere out at sea. Maggie and Tully's boss, Assistant Director Raymond Kunze, who never met a politician he couldn't be manipulated by, had sent his two agents to play fetch.

Okay, that wasn't at all how Kunze had worded it, of course, but that was what it felt like to Maggie and Tully.

Kunze had been sending the two of them on odd missions for about two years now. And just when Maggie thought the shelf life on his reign of punishment would expire, he came up with yet another assignment or errand.

The storm added urgency to their mission. Maggie and Tully had barely escaped DC before the snow began falling. But they hadn't escaped the storm front. The monster system looped all the way down from the Midwest to the Panhandle of Florida then back up the eastern coastline.

Down here in Florida it was only just beginning, taking the form of angry, black thunderheads. It had rained all the way from the airport. Seventeen to twenty inches were predicted during the next forty-eight hours. They were in a lull. In the distance Maggie could hear a rumble of thunder, a reminder that the calm would not last long. As if on queue, the pilot, Lieutenant Commander Wilson, gestured for her to hurry up and come aboard. Then he climbed inside.

Liz Bailey, the rescue swimmer, and Pete Kesnik, the

flight mechanic, both waited for her at the cabin door. Bailey had already slipped Maggie a couple of capsules when no one was watching. She had done this favor for Maggie the last time even before she knew her. Who would have guessed it would become a ritual.

The capsules were a concoction of ginger and other herbs that magically quelled her nausea. Maggie dry-swallowed them now. Then she put on her flight helmet and climbed into the helicopter.

Chapter 2

THE WIND WHIPPED AND SHOVED at the Coast Guard H-65 Helo. Bruise-colored clouds threatened to burst. Maggie could see flickers of lightning rippling through the mass that, thankfully, continued to stay in the distance for now. But it was definitely moving their way. It looked like the storm was rolling in on waves of clouds and in layers of gray and purple. Below, the gulf water swirled and churned up white caps.

Sane people would be starting to take shelter, moving inland and grounding their flights in preparation for the storm. Wind gusts of forty to sixty miles per hour were predicted along with the rain. Yet, this aircrew had not flinched at the order to take flight.

Within fifteen minutes they found what they believed to be the senator's houseboat. Maggie knew from the file she and Tully had been given that the boat was eighteen feet wide by seventy-five feet long. It was a luxury widebody named *Electric Blue* and worth almost a half million dollars. From two-hundred feet above it looked like a toy rocking and rolling in a sea of boiling water.

Maggie watched Liz Bailey prepare to deploy. No one else appeared to think this was an absolutely crazy idea. Wilson and his co-pilot, Tommy Ellis, couldn't keep the helicopter from pitching one way and jerking the other as they tried to hover above the boat. And yet, Bailey was going to leap out into the gusts, tethered to the helicopter by a single cable. Maggie had watched her do it before but it still astonished her. Was it bravery or insanity?

Maggie had been impressed with the young woman from the moment they met. Liz—Elizabeth Bailey, AST3, RS (rescue swimmer)—was a Coastie veteran at twenty-eight years old. She had told Maggie stories about how she had scraped her knees on sinking rooftops during Katrina and waded through debris-filled sewage left by Isaac. Despite having more rescues than many of her male counterparts Bailey was still considered a novelty, a rare breed, one of less than a dozen women to pass the rigorous training and earn the title "rescue swimmer."

That was one thing she and Maggie had in common. Both of them had clawed their way to garnering respect in fields that were still male dominated. But Bailey had done so under extreme circumstances, propelling herself out into the elements, literally hanging by what Maggie considered a thread. Having watched her do that a few times, Maggie was convinced she had the less dangerous job of hunting killers.

Now Bailey was ready. She sidled up to the cabin door but she had put off changing out her flight helmet with ICS for her Seda swim helmet. Maggie knew she was waiting while her aircrew tried to assess the situation below. Once she switched out helmets she would no longer be able to communicate with them except through hand signals.

"No one's responding," Tommy Ellis, their co-pilot said. He had been trying to make radio contact with the houseboat.

"Keep trying." Lt. Commander Wilson told him. "Who the hell takes a houseboat out in the Gulf of Mexico with a monster storm in the forecast?"

"It was supposed to be just a few thunderstorms," Pete Kesnick said, while he checked the cables.

Kesnick, the flight mechanic was also the hoist operator. Maggie remembered that he was the senior member of this aircrew with fifteen or sixteen years, all of them at Air Station Mobile.

"Ever been on one before?" Kesnick asked no one in particular. "Like a floating condo. Pretty sweet." He adjusted and worked the cables that would lower Bailey down.

Wilson slid back his flight helmet's visor and turned to look at Bailey. He waited for her eyes before he said, "I don't like this. Dispatch claims six on board. We can't rouse anyone and I sure as hell don't see anybody."

The last time Maggie had been on board with this crew the men had all but ignored Bailey. Sometime during a nasty rescue flight in the vicious outer bands of Hurricane Isaac, Maggie had watched this same aircrew go from calling Liz Bailey "*the* rescue swimmer" to "*our* rescue swimmer." She was glad to see the attitude had stuck.

From what Maggie knew there had been no distress call from the boat. That was one of the reasons the senator had gone into full panic mode. And Wilson was right. Maggie couldn't see anyone down below. Empty lounge chairs and a putting green that looked the size of a postage stamp occupied the upper deck. The lower couldn't be seen from above, but if anyone was on board and the radio was out, they'd be coming out into view, at least, to take a look at the noise above.

Instead, the houseboat thrashed around as waves pummeled against its sides. It made no attempt to escape or retreat. Maggie was definitely no expert but she couldn't help wondering if the engines had been turned off and the steering house abandoned. Interior lights could be seen, but may have been automatically powered on by the darkening sky.

"It's your call, Bailey," Wilson finally said. "What say you?"

Chapter 3

R.J. TULLY THOUGHT HE HAD THE easy part of this assignment until he met Senator Ellie Delanor-Ramos.

She had asked to meet him in the parking lot under Pensacola Beach's famous beach ball water tower. Most of the spaces were empty. Still, he chose a corner closest to the water. He had seen the junior senator from Florida in newspaper photos and on television news. She had become an outspoken proponent for immigration reform though pundits were always quick to point out that her own ancestry traced back to the Mayflower. She was hardly the poster child for such an endeavor and even her physical presence seemed to highlight that fact.

A strikingly beautiful woman in her forties, her skin was creamy white, her eyes a bright blue. She wore her mane of caramel-colored hair loose and just long enough to brush her shoulders when she walked. As Tully watched her cross the parking lot, flanked by two men, he understood immediately why this woman was regarded as one of the most powerful women in Washington, D.C. She carried herself not at all like the model or beauty queen that she looked like, but rather a Fortune 500 CEO, one capable of shoving aside or destroying anything – or anyone – who might stand in her way.

"You must be Agent Tully," she said with her hand outstretched to him from four feet away.

"That's correct, Senator." Her grip was firm, long fingers, nails painted a blood red.

"For God's sake, call my Ellie."

"Are you sure?"

"Absolutely. Do you prefer R.J. or Agent Tully?"

"Actually just Tully is fine."

He glanced at the two men who accompanied her. No introductions were expected. Both men stood silent and a foot behind her. Secret Service? Bodyguards? They wore dark suits and sunglasses despite the gray sky. They looked more like federal agents than Tully did.

"I missed the helicopter?" she asked an obvious question immediately betraying her cool, calm façade.

"I'm afraid so."

"Any news?"

It had been less than thirty minutes. And Tully was certain the senator would be alerted of any news long before he would, just like she knew the helicopter had already left.

Instead of answering and wasting time with pleasantries, he said, "Sheriff Langley said there was someplace you wanted me to check out."

"Yes, but I don't want that idiot going along."

So much for pleasantries. "Sheriff Langley?"

"If I thought the locals could handle this I wouldn't have asked Raymond for his assistance."

"Raymond," Tully realized was FBI Assistant Director Kunze – his boss. It sounded odd having someone call him by his first name. A little like calling Hitler, "Adolf." It made Tully even more uncomfortable going over the heads of local law enforcement. This was their turf, their territory. Forget about pissing contests. Usually it made sense to have them leading the way, or at least along for the ride. Local law enforcement had the contacts. They knew the players as well as the shortcuts. It saved time. Mostly, it spared Tully from a lot of headaches. But this was a United States senator. Both he and Maggie had been told to "assist her" in any way possible that would return her family safely ashore.

"Where is it that you want me check?"

"A friend of my husband's." She hesitated, looking for the correct word. "Not really a friend. More of a business associate."

"What exactly to do you think happened here?"

She glanced back at the two men. "Can we have some privacy, please?"

The bigger one nodded and gestured to the other. But they didn't go far.

"Not my idea," she told Tully, her eyes darting back to the men to indicate it was them she was talking about.

"From what I understand, your husband simply took your houseboat out for a ride. Your husband and your children—two, right?"

She nodded and Tully could immediately see just the mention of the kids caused a reaction. There was a shift in her posture, her shoulders actually slumped forward if only for a moment or two, as though she had been carrying a heavy weight and just remembered it was still there. Her eye contact had been piercing but now there was a flicker in the brilliant blue that betrayed the fatigue, maybe even a hint of panic.

"George builds boats for a living. He built our houseboat. And he can certainly handle it on stormy waters."

"This was supposed to be a family outing?"

"Yes. I was meeting them but I got delayed." Her eyes slipped past Tully and past the parking lot toward the emerald green water of the Gulf.

Tully studied her face, thought he saw regret. He could tell it wasn't the first time she had been late for a family outing. Maybe her husband was driving home that point. Teaching her a lesson. Tully's ex-wife used to work late all the time. She'd cancel out on him and his daughter Emma constantly, so much so that after the divorce he and Emma hardly missed her at all.

Pensacola Beach had quieted in the time since Tully and Maggie arrived. A few tourists were still out on the beach. Despite the red flag, a couple of daredevil surfers were riding the waves. Others had gone indoors. Tully could see a full deck at the restaurant, Crabs. The dark sky had even set off the parking lot lights.

For as much as the senator appeared in a hurry, now she seemed contemplative, still watching the gulf as if she hoped to see the houseboat crest over the next set of waves. Tully couldn't imagine George Ramos taking his kids out with a monster storm coming even if he thought he could teach his senator wife a lesson. But then Tully had seen people do a lot of strange things to each other. Still, he knew when to keep his mouth shut. She must have suspected what he was thinking.

"I know something's terribly wrong," she said.

Finally she looked at Tully, met his gaze. There was a firm resolve in her eyes but he caught a glint of sadness before she could stow it away. "And they wouldn't have left without me."

Chapter 4

BY MAGGIE'S CALCULATIONS Liz Bailey had been down on the houseboat for nine minutes. Shouldn't that be enough time to know if anyone was aboard? If there were injuries? Whether or not they needed to send down the rescue basket or the medavac board?

"Have you seen her yet?" Wilson asked Kesnick for the third time.

"Nothing yet."

"Where the hell's that cutter?"

"They said less than an hour," Tommy Ellis told him.

Wilson shook his head in exaggerated frustration. But Maggie understood. An hour seemed like forever.

To make matters worse, the rain had started. Not a few raindrops or a light shower but a torrential downpour. The helicopter rocked and jerked despite Wilson's best efforts. Maggie's heart thump-thumped against her ribcage with the rhythm of the rotors. Sweat trickled down her back. The helmet threatened to suffocate her. She pushed back the visor. It didn't help.

Fortunately, she was too concerned about Bailey to pay attention to the churning in her stomach. Each jolt of the helicopter sent new spasms of nausea. She tasted blood before she realized she was biting down on her lower lip.

"Is she still with us?" Wilson wanted to know.

Kesnick pulled on the cable till it was taut. He had slowly let out sections, a little at a time as Bailey moved from the top deck to the bottom and then as she disappeared inside. Now he nodded to Wilson when he seemed convinced that she was still attached.

"Give her a tug."

"I have already."

"Visibility is turning to crap," Tommy Ellis said. "Pretty soon we won't be able to see her."

"We can't be out here much longer," Wilson told them. "I'm gonna take us down closer. Kesnick keep an eye out."

Maggie white-knuckled the straps on the side of the helicopter. Wilson's attempt to lower the craft met resistance. The wind gusts grabbed them, rocking and swaying every inch. Then suddenly they dropped. A freefall.

"Son of a bitch." Wilson wrestled them back from a roller coaster plunge.

Maggie's holstered revolver dug into her side and she realized how totally defenseless she felt. The void of control overwhelmed her. It wasn't motion sickness. It was the inability to do anything but sit back.

"I see her," Kesnick yelled as he slid his visor up for a better look. "She's waving from the lower deck."

"What does she need?"

Maggie watched Kesnick's face. Tanned and weathered. Crinkle lines at the eyes. Not an easy read. The man kept his expressions intact but this time she saw his eyes go wide.

"She's telling us to back away."

"What the hell?"

Maggie scooted along the side of the cabin as far as her seat belt would allow. She craned her neck and she could see Bailey leaning over the railing. Her right arm was raised with an open palm like she was waving at them but instead she pumped her hand back and forth.

Just as suddenly as the downpour began, it lightened. Even the helicopter steadied to a sway. Bailey could be seen more clearly and there was no mistaking her meticulous, slow but persistent hand signals.

"Do you see anyone else?" Wilson asked.

Kesnick shifted and twisted. So did Maggie.

"Could be someone inside. But I don't see anybody."

And Bailey didn't give anything away. If someone was threatening her and telling her to send her flight crew away, she wasn't looking to him.

"Maybe there's something on board," Kesnick said. "Explosives?"

"Then she needs to get her ass back up here. Now. Pull her up."

Maggie noticed a new hand signal just as Kesnick grabbed at the cable. He noticed, too, and stopped.

"Wait. There's more."

Bailey was grasping her clenched fist then pulling and separating.

"She's disconnecting from the hoist hook," Kesnick said and Maggie heard the panic in his voice.

"Son of a bitch." Wilson yelled. "Don't let her do it, Kesnick. Pull her ass up. Get her the hell out of there."

Kesnick scrambled to get his feet set. Then he double-fisted the cable, but Maggie could see it was too late. Bailey had already disconnected and the cable spun free.

Kesnick fell backwards. "Damn it!"

Wilson and Ellis both twisted around in their seats, but they wouldn't be able to see out the cabin window or door from their seats at the controls. Still, Maggie saw the stunned looks on their faces.

Kesnick scooted back into position.

"She's pushing us off again," he told the others.

Then Maggie saw Bailey raise her arm straight up, open palm facing forward.

"She's signaling that she's alright," Kesnick translated.

Bailey's arm stayed up.

"Maybe she just wants us to get out of the weather," Tommy Ellis said.

Maggie didn't think he sounded convincing though the storm was beginning to intensify again.

The wind gusted and sent the helicopter rocking. Another layer of dark clouds rolled in over them, this time flickering with streaks of lightning. Thunder rumbled and Maggie could feel its vibration against her back.

"Yeah, we've got to head back before we get knocked out of the sky."

"You can't just leave her," Maggie said.

The men went quiet. It was her first sentence since they had left the beach. Kesnick concentrated on Bailey whose arm was still raised.

"You know the rules, O'Dell. None of us are allowed to deploy except the rescue swimmer."

Yes, she did remember Wilson telling her that the last time.

"My job is to make sure the family on that houseboat returns safely to shore," she told them.

"A cutter's on its way," Ellis repeated.

"Something's wrong." It was Kesnick.

Maggie turned to look back down at Bailey. Her right arm was still raised but now she was waving it from side to side, a brisk, forceful wave.

"What is she telling us?" Maggie demanded when Kesnick failed to relay the message. "What does that mean?"

"Emergency," Kesnick said. "Needs assistance." He turned to Wilson. "She's in trouble."

"I'm going down." Maggie had already unhooked her seat belt and was sliding over to Kesnick.

"Like hell you are." But Wilson was struggling to keep the helicopter steady. Rain lashed at the sides.

Kesnick started preparing the cable. Maggie had done this before but somehow that didn't make it easier. She relied on adrenaline to push her toward the cabin door.

"You have no authority, O'Dell. This is my aircraft."

"You have no authority over me, Commander Wilson. That boat down there is the only reason I'm here. And something's going on whether we can see it or not."

"No one deploys except the rescue swimmer. Those are the rules, O'Dell."

"I've never been very good at following rules."

Maggie yanked off her helmet to end any further discussion. Without the helmet and ICS, she wouldn't be able to hear Wilson. It didn't stop him from yelling at her. But Kesnick was already helping her. He handed her a Seda lightweight helmet, just like the one Bailey wore. Maggie pulled it on and didn't bother to tuck her hair up into it.

Kesnick reached around her, looping and securing the harness. He positioned the quick strop over her shoulders, showing her – reminding her – how to work it and where to hold on. She snapped the goggles into place. Then she tested her gloved hands on the cable and realized she must be completely out of her mind.

She looked directly into Kesnick's eyes and saw his intensity. He leaned into her and yelled, "Let me do all the heavy lifting. You just hang on. I'll get you down."

But they both knew she wouldn't be coming back up.

He tapped her on the chest, two fingers right below her collarbone, just like he had with Bailey. The universal signal for "ready." She gave him a thumbs up and slid herself out of the helicopter door.

Almost immediately Maggie went into a spin, a dizzy, wild ride. She tucked her chin and dug her heels together so the cable wouldn't wrap around her neck. The wind was heartless and only accelerated the spinning. Rain pelted her. The thump-thump of the rotors continued to compete with her heart. Thunder roared above. Or at least she thought it was thunder. It was difficult to distinguish.

Her goggles clouded with the spray of rain. It didn't

matter. She had her eyes squeezed tight. She knew if she opened them it would only add to the dizziness. She waited for the spinning to stop but even as Kesnick lowered her, it continued.

After what seemed like an eternity, her heels connected with something more solid than air. Maggie opened her eyes. Through the blur of her goggles she saw the upper deck of the houseboat. She pushed off and swung herself to the lower deck, sliding past the railing.

She felt Bailey's hands before she really saw the woman. Bailey pulled her down and helped disconnect her. She seemed in a hurry. The noise of the helicopter, the storm and the waves hitting the boat filled Maggie's ears and even when Bailey's mouth moved, Maggie couldn't make out the words. But she looked worried and frantic.

Maggie yanked the goggles down in time to see the cable – their only connection to the outside world – zip back up to the helicopter. Bailey was gesturing to them. The same signals, one after another. Telling them to back away, followed by "I'm alright" then immediately contradicting herself with the signal for "emergency, in trouble."

Maggie tried to understand, tried to catch Bailey's eyes. As she glanced away for an answer she suddenly saw a man underneath the deck's awning, hidden from view of the helicopter. He was on the far end of the houseboat but Maggie could still see what he held on his shoulder. Even in the blur of wind and rain she knew exactly what it was. He was aiming an RPG right at the helicopter.

Chapter 5

TULLY CHECKED HIS MESSAGES. He had texted Sheriff Langley about Maggie's Coast Guard crew. Surely there had been some word radioed in from them. But the latest response from the sheriff was annoyingly short: NOTHING.

How could there be nothing? That was bullshit!

Tully waited in his rental. He sat facing the Gulf, shifting his eyes from the black rolling mass of clouds that flickered with electricity to watching in his rearview mirror as the senator talked to her personal men-in-black. The clouds had turned day into night.

He tried calling Sheriff Langley for a second time, but the call went directly to voice mail. The sheriff would be pissed if he discovered Senator Delanor Ramos had passed on even a courtesy meeting with him. Was he pissed enough to withhold information? And why didn't she understand this? Wouldn't she want every possible law enforcement officer working to help? Or was it more important to keep the truth from getting out? Everything was political, either an asset or liability. Was the truth a liability in this case?

Something had obviously happened to her family. Maybe their houseboat simply broke down along with the radio. Could that happen with a half-million dollar boat? But she didn't believe it was that simple. She'd said as much.

He ran a hand through his hair. Now he could see the sheet of white under the clouds. In minutes that sheet of rain would be on top of them. He sent another text to Maggie. None had been answered. He didn't expect this one to be either, but he had to keep trying.

The passenger door opened and Senator Delanor Ramos hopped up and into the seat. She shoved an oversized tote onto the floormat beside her feet and buckled herself in, getting comfortable like she was going to spend an afternoon sightseeing. Tully craned his neck to see what her bodyguards were doing. If he wasn't mistaken, the black Escalade wasn't waiting on them.

She saw him looking in the rearview mirror and before he could ask, she said, "They would have only gotten in the way." Already she looked relieved.

And suddenly Tully realized that this was more serious than he thought. She was narrowing down her liabilities to just him. The fewer people who knew, the better.

What the hell was going on?

If his family were missing out at sea he would be calling in the cavalry, wanting all available personnel helping. Instead, the senator was counting on two FBI agents and one Coast Guard aircrew.

"You never answered my question," Tully said. "What exactly do you suspect has happened?"

"Agent Tully . . . Tully," she corrected herself even as she lightened her tone. After all, she was stuck with only him. "If I knew what happened to my family I wouldn't need the FBI, would I?"

"You obviously have some idea or you'd simply let the Coast Guard handle it."

He glanced over, but her face was turned to the window.

"I fear there's nothing simple about this."

He noticed her hands. While the rest of her body looked calm and under control, the fingers of her right hand twisted and turned her wedding ring, tugging it up over her knuckle only to shove it back down and start again.

Chapter 6

MAGGIE RIPPED AT THE FLIGHT SUIT'S zipper. Without being told, she knew the man with the rocket launcher on his shoulder was not the only terrorist on board. She needed to disarm herself before they did it for her. Bailey immediately saw what Maggie was doing and moved her body, but she wasn't just trying to block Maggie from the view of the man on deck. Bailey was also trying to stand in front of the window.

So someone else was there, watching. Of course, they were.

They'd needed to stay out of sight until the helicopter left. And Bailey's hand signals were supposed to accomplish that. No wonder the woman was so determined to get them to back off. The choice presented to her must have been to make the helicopter disappear or they would do it with a rocket. But they weren't versed in Coast Guard hand signals. They had no idea that while Bailey had told her aircrew to back off and that all was fine, she had also told them there was an emergency and that she was in trouble.

Maggie caught Bailey's eyes. They darted toward the boat and the window behind her. Then she blinked once, twice, three times. So there were three of them.

Maggie glanced over Bailey's shoulder to the man with the rocket then back at Bailey. She didn't know how to ask if he was included in the three. Before she could figure it out, Bailey gave a slight nod. Then her eyes darted down to the deck floor at Maggie's feet.

It looked like an oversized tackle box attached to the deck with metal brackets. A bungee cord kept it shut. Maggie tucked her hands inside of her flight suit though she had unzipped it to her waist. Her fingers tugged her shoulder holster free but like her hands, she held it hidden inside the suit.

When the next set of waves crashed up over the deck, the boat tipped and Maggie went down to her knees, pretending to lose her balance. Bailey teetered in front of her, arms outstretched as she grabbed the railing on one side and the wall with the other. She provided the perfect barricade.

Maggie grabbed at the bungee cord. She pulled up and slid the holster with the revolver into the tackle box in one quick motion, letting it slam shut. There was no relief watching her only control, her only hope of defense, disappear out of sight. Before she stood back up another wave knocked her back to her knees. She look up at Bailey and saw the young woman's eyes trying to get her attention as she tapped her chest. When Maggie didn't understand, Bailey pricked at the emblem on her dive suit and pointed with her chin at Maggie then at the tackle box.

Her FBI badge. Of course. Bailey wanted her to dump it in the box. Maggie's fingers fished back into her flight suit, found the wallet and shoved it in under the lid.

The thunderclouds had been roaring overhead with lightning streaks that seemed to crackle. Waves swished and rain pelted the aluminum sides of the boat making it sound like a tin can being used as target practice for an AK-47. But the sound that drew Maggie's attention and sent her pulse into a panic was the helicopter leaving. The sound of the rotor wash lifted. The engine noise reduced to a hum, fading fast. And then it was swallowed up in the reverberation of the storm.

Their lifeline. *Gone.*

Chapter 7

TULLY TRIED TO PAY ATTENTION to the street signs—at least the ones he could make out through the downpour—even though he followed Senator Delanor Ramos directions. They had gone over two long bridges in blinding rain while the water churned below. Traffic had slowed down to twenty miles per hour. Tully tight-fisted the SUV's steering wheel, fighting against the wind gusts. They were on Scenic Highway now, a long winding two-lane that ran parallel to one of the bays.

"This associate," Tully said, "we couldn't just call him?" He had to raise his voice over the accelerated squeak-and-slash of the windshield wipers. The rain pelted the vehicle's roof.

"I tried. It went directly to voice mail."

In the streetlights and headlights Tully could see water rushing over the highway. Red taillights winked up ahead and he pumped the brakes slowly to avoid locking them up. It looked like there were broken branches covering one lane of traffic. Huge live oaks grew on the bluffs, the area between the highway and the water. Branches overhung the road in places.

"Tell me about this business associate," Tully said. He felt like he was yelling over the pounding of rain.

"They used to be partners."

"Building boats?"

"Yes. But Ricardo isn't a builder. Or a designer. I doubt that he could build a doghouse."

She was wringing her hands again. Glanced at her wristwatch and checked her cell phone. Just the reminder of Ricardo's incompetence – or maybe it was only the debris in the road – seemed to make her restless.

He could tell she was trying to decide how much to tell him.

"He helped with the financing." Another pause. "Building boats is expensive – materials, labor. Sometimes clients pay at different stages of completion. Sometimes they pay upon delivery."

There was something about the way she talked about her husband's business, and not just Ricardo, that made Tully realize she didn't approve.

"So Ricardo is rich?" he asked.

The senator burst out laughing. She had to wipe tears from her eyes and shook her head as if it was the most ridiculous thing she had heard.

"No," she finally managed. "Ricardo is not rich. He's a big talker. He missed his calling. Ricardo should have been a politician."

"You don't sound like you approved of their partnership."

"No, I didn't. They grew up together in the slums of Bogota. Ricardo's not even family but George is constantly looking after him. Bailing him out. Whenever there's trouble I know where to look because it usually has something to do Ricardo."

It was their turn to use the single lane and Tully eased the SUV around the debris. The branch had taken some electrical lines with it. Water was running across the highway, almost to the chassis of the sedan in front of him. He was grateful he'd insisted on an SUV. Still, it was crazy to be out visiting old partners. He wanted to be back at the air station waiting for word on Maggie and her crew. Maybe they had already found the houseboat. How far out could a boat like that go in weather like this?

"How much farther is it?" he asked her, not bothering to keep his impatience from his voice.

"Not far. About another mile and then a left on Creighton. It's just a few blocks up from there."

The bungalow set back from the street. The detached garage was obviously added, almost as large as the house. Up and down the street Tully could see house lights on, families staying inside and taking shelter from the storm. The storm drains couldn't keep up with the rain that still came down in sheets. Water gushed over the curbs, flooding lawns and driveways.

Tully pulled the SUV as close to the house as possible but there was already a Jeep parked in front of the garage. It would still be a jog to the front door. By the time he got under the small awning he'd be drenched. Senator Delanor Ramos must have been thinking the same thing. She was pulling out an umbrella from her tote bag. When she reached for the door handle he realized she expected to go with him.

"Wait. Why don't you stay here? I'll see if he's even home."

She looked back at the house and seemed to consider this. Electrical lines danced above and tree branches creaked. Tully could see a faint light behind the tightly drawn blinds. But that was it.

He didn't wait for a response. He wanted to get this over with. He opened the SUV's door and leaped out, slamming the door as he took off in a sprint. The water ran ankle deep in places, covering the front lawn. If there was a sidewalk, Tully couldn't see it.

Thunder rumbled overhead and in the flashes of lightning he thought he saw someone standing in the trees alongside the house. It was enough for him to grab inside his

Windbreaker for his Glock. But when he finally made it under the front door's awning he couldn't see anyone.

Was the wind and rain playing tricks on his eyesight? He wiped a hand over his face and his head swiveled around, trying to take in the yard and street and the narrow passage between the house and garage.

But there was no one. No pedestrians, no cars. Not even farther up the street.

Tully knocked on the door just as the thunder clashed. He waited and knocked again, harder. He tried the doorknob and to his surprise it turned. He eased the door open with one hand and gripped his weapon in the other.

"Hello? Mr. Ricardo?"

He noticed the flies first. Swarms of them in the faint light of table lamp. Then he noticed the smell.

Tully slowly entered. His eyes darted everywhere as he took small steps, his weapon drawn and leading. He didn't need to go far when he saw the living room's back wall. Warm sunshine yellow sprayed and splattered with blood.

"Oh my God."

He heard the senator behind him in the doorway. Tully threw out his left hand.

"Stay back," he warned as he continued farther inside. Right around the wide archway door he found the body slumped against the refrigerator. The man was in his underwear. His right kneecap was blown away as were several of his fingers. But the deathblow was a single shot to the forehead.

It looked like Ricardo hadn't been able to talk his way out of this one.

Chapter 8

THE MAN WITH THE RPG was named Diego. The one on the other side of the window with the AK-47 was Felipe. Not that they formally introduced themselves to Maggie and Liz. They spoke Spanish to each other but surprisingly good English to their hostages. The fact that they were comfortable using each other's name in front of them, kicked Maggie's heartbeat up a notch. They didn't mind Maggie and Liz knowing because they didn't expect their two intruders to tell anyone . . . ever.

Now that the helicopter was gone the two men had forced Maggie and Liz inside the boat. Liz's dive suit left little room for concealing weapons. Immediately the smaller of the two, Felipe, unzipped Maggie's flight suit and raced his hands over her body. She fought her basic instinct to punch away. Thankfully he was in a hurry so his fingers poked and prodded without little attempt at being salacious.

It was a relief of sorts just to get out of the storm. Her hair was dripping, her adrenaline still racing. Her nerves left raw from spinning on the cable ride down. She made herself take deep breaths to steady herself, but the air inside smelled stale. Stale with a metallic tang and the hint of cordite. They had obviously interrupted something.

The dark paneled walls muffled the thunder and rain to a

battering but there was nothing to shut off the sway. The boat was large enough that when the waves pushed and shoved, the boat didn't jerk. It rolled, tipping and tilting one way until it threatened to send everything and everyone sliding. Then slowly it crested over a swell, heaved a sigh and began tipping in the other direction.

Diego had exchanged his RPG for an automatic handgun. Maggie felt it in the small of her back as he prodded her forward, at times almost pushing her into Liz. Felipe led them through the narrow hallway. Polished cherry wood rose from floor to ceiling broken up only by the living room's bookcases and bar, and the kitchen's stainless-steel appliances and granite countertops. No cost had been spared. And although glassware rattled and wine bottles clinked against each other, everything appeared to be staying in place despite the motion.

As they passed closed doors Maggie tried to listen for sounds of life. They were told there were six on board including the senator's teenaged daughter, her eight-year old son and her husband. If this was an abduction, they had to be here somewhere. Hopefully unharmed.

Perhaps Felipe read her mind. At the next door he stopped. He grinned back at Diego and said something Maggie didn't understand. Their Spanish was different somehow. Not what she was used to.

Diego laughed and Felipe pushed the door open, making sure it swung wide enough for them to see inside. He gestured for Liz to take a look but he was showing off, not asking for them to go into the room. Maggie saw Liz's shoulders drop but she managed to mask her emotions.

Then it was time for Maggie's sneak peek. And Felipe was anxious, the grin never leaving his face. Inside the laundry room three bodies were sprawled out on top of each other, purposely stacked to accommodate the small space. At the top of the heap, a woman laid with her back arched, flopped over the other two. Her head and shoulders faced the doorway only she stared wide-eyed at them from upside down. The bullet hole in her forehead still oozed.

So here was the crew. And Maggie understood clearly what Felipe was telling her and Liz. He wasn't just showing off their handiwork. He was telling Maggie and Liz that they would soon be joining the pile.

Chapter 9

TULLY HAD INSTRUCTED THE SENATOR to go back and stay in the SUV. To his surprise, she had obeyed without argument or discussion. Despite how tough the woman was, he knew the scene inside Ricardo's house was not something she had ever experienced before. And although she had been withholding information and dealing it out piecemeal to Tully since the minute they met, he also knew, that she had not expected or even suspected this.

The most frustrating part for Tully? Not fifteen minutes after finding Ricardo, the senator's political instinct already started kicking into gear. As soon as Tully jumped back into the SUV she was insisting they leave.

"A patrol unit is on the way," Tully explained.

"I can't be here when they arrive."

He looked over at her but she was staring ahead through the blurred windshield. The streetlights cast her face in shadow.

"Are you suggesting I leave the scene?"

"You've reported it, correct? It's not like we can tell them anything."

Which wasn't entirely true. He knew there was plenty the senator could tell the local law enforcement about

Ricardo that they might never know.

"I've already called Raymond." And she said this as though she was pulling rank on him. "He understands the situation. He told me he'd take care of things."

Tully saw that she had her cell phone clutched tightly in her hand. The faceplate was still lit. For a woman who was careful and deliberate about her every move and concerned about her actions recorded and accounted for, he knew that her call to the FBI assistant director had been an added risk.

"Where do you suggest we go from here?"

"Back to the beach."

"Another business associate?"

"No," she said, but she winced as though his sarcasm had struck a nerve. "A friend."

It took them forever to backtrack. More branches were down. The water rushed across streets and in places so high that it looked as if it swallowed the tires of small sedans. Many were stranded along the sides. But it didn't seem to stop people from venturing out. There was still a remarkable amount of traffic.

Once they crossed the bridge and were back on the beach, the senator pointed to a marina on the gulf side.

"I'm hoping Howard will have something more to tell us."

"Howard is the friend?"

She nodded.

"Yours or your husband's?"

"Both. But he knows George. He's known him for a very long time."

"Like Ricardo?"

"No, not like Ricardo. Not at all like Ricardo." She shook her head as if she was trying to forget the image. "Howard is a friend. And we keep our houseboat here."

"So Howard may have seen them leave?"

"Howard would never let George take a boat out in weather like this, especially with the kids."

"Would he have stopped George?"

She seemed to consider this for a beat too long then said, "I doubt it. When George puts his mind to something there usually is no further discussion."

Tully pulled up as close as he could to the shop. The rain continued, drumming down and interspersed with wind gusts that sent the rain horizontal in violent blasts. Thunder shook the vehicle. Lightning streaked through the sky tinting the world a neon blue and crackling like electrical sparks.

The two-story shop had a marlin painted on the side and orange and blue letters that read: Howard Johnson's Deep-Sea Fishing. Beside it was Bobbye's Oyster Bar. Both looked closed though there was a faint light on in the shop.

Bistro tables were shoved against the bar's south wall. Chairs were turned over and stacked securely on top of the tables then chained down. Still, the wind rattled the cast iron. Across the boardwalk boats of all sizes rocked in their slips and lurched against their tie-down lines.

Though she still had the umbrella in her hand Senator Delanor Ramos made no attempt to open it. They were both soaking wet. Still, she carried it as she ran for cover under the shop's awning. A graceful run, almost a prance – Ginger Rogers in three-inch heels. Tully followed, his size thirteen's finding puddles already deep enough to swallow his loafers. Gwen would kill him. She had bought him the Italian leather shoes for one of their anniversaries. How awful was it that he couldn't remember which anniversary? And then, even through the crashes of thunder, without his mind missing a beat, he immediately thought – how awful was it that your significant other bought you shoes for an anniversary? It was a crazy thing to think about on a night like this one. But it was a crazy night.

To his surprise the shop door opened despite the CLOSED sign in the window. A huge man stood behind the counter, towering over it. Barreled chested with muscular arms. He wore a bright colored boat shirt and white linen trousers. His thick hair was completely white as was his mustache and wide sideburns, although he didn't look older than sixty.

The only light in the shop came from inside the display cases and a neon sign – another marlin – this one, brilliant green and yellow. The neon danced in the reflection of the glass cases. Along with the lightning, it cast the entire shop in an otherworld illumination. Tully couldn't help thinking the man looked more like a captain of a spaceship rather than a deep-sea fishing boat.

"Can I help you folks?" he asked before he looked up. The baritone voice was kind and gentle despite the fact that he already had closed for the day. When he did look up, he had to do a double take. As soon as he recognized the senator he smiled – bright white teeth and laugh lines – and he shook his head. "Ellie, what in the world are you doing out in weather like this?"

He didn't wait for her reply. He came around the counter and engulfed her in a hug.

The tough-as-nails powerbroker of a senator, hugged him tight, standing on tip-toe to do it, and when he let her go, Tully saw her swat tears from her eyes.

"Howard, it's good to see you."

"I saw the boat was gone," he said before the question was asked. "What is George up to this time?"

Chapter 10

"JORGE, HERE ARE THE VISITORS", Felipe called out.

Diego had stayed back at the laundry room while Felipe had shoved Maggie and Liz forward onto a deck that was glassed in and protected from the storm. Even in the dark Maggie could see the waves crashing up and over the outside railings. She recognized it as the steering cabin of the boat.

A dark-haired man sat in the captain chair behind the steering wheel and in front of a panel of instruments. He glanced over his shoulder but only briefly. His attention stayed focused on the instruments that were barely lit.

Maggie had felt the engine come to life as they were walking through the narrow hallway. The vibration had rumbled under their feet and she knew the boat was moving again. She tried to remember what Tommy Ellis had said about the Coast Guard cutter. It was less than an hour away. How long ago was that? If the houseboat started moving in the opposite direction would the cutter ever find it? She wanted to ask Liz. She tried to read the younger woman's expression now that she was able to see her face.

Felipe motioned for them to sit on one of the benches alongside the wall. When Maggie didn't comply quickly enough he shoved her down. The man behind the steering wheel turned and scowled at him.

"Really, Felipe?"

"What? They are federales."

"Yes, and if you kill one of them this will be the end."

From Maggie's angle she could see Diego. He was dragging one of the bodies from the laundry room out onto to the deck. Somehow he worked the rocking of the boat and wind to his advantage. Instead of struggling, he waited for the tilt then raised the body up and let the wind and waves push it over the railing.

Maggie looked away, biting back the anger and helplessness she was feeling. Her mind tried to work the pieces together. Initially when she saw the RPG she thought terrorists had pirated the boat. It made sense. Senator Delanor Ramos was a powerful and outspoken political official. But political motivation seemed to drift away the more she watched the two thugs. Though perhaps Jorge was their mastermind.

Revenge or kidnapping seemed more likely. The houseboat was clearly luxurious. She had no idea of the senator's financial situation but a ransom would fit the profile of men like Diego and Felipe.

Then into this macabre nightmare a little boy wandered in from a doorway at the opposite end. He was dressed in baggy shorts and an Angry Birds T-shirt. He ignored the rest of them and ran to the man at the helm.

"Daddy, Angelica is hogging the X-box."

The man patted the boy and pulled him up onto his lap. Maggie exchanged a stunned look with Liz. She couldn't believe it. Jorge was George Ramos.

Chapter 11

TULLY FIDGETED WHILE HOWARD pulled out an expensive looking bottle of liquor. He set three crystal-cut rocks glasses on a bistro table in the corner of the shop. As Tully wandered over he noticed the shelf that ran a foot below the high ceiling. It lined all four walls and displayed miniature model boats, tightly packed, end-to-end. They were the type that someone painstakingly had put together and painted, delicate lines and tiny pieces. He couldn't help glancing at Howard's large hands. They looked more like they belonged to a boxer than a man who applied fine details to tiny bits of plastic.

The senator had just told Howard about Ricardo. Tully couldn't help noticing that he didn't look shocked, not even surprised. Those big hands were steady and graceful as he poured the amber liquid. He slid a glass in front of the senator then set down a second one for Tully before he filled his own glass.

"Some of the old dogs have come sniffing around again in the last couple of years." He told the senator as he glanced from her to Tully then back.

"Oh, it's okay, Howard. He's one of Raymond's agents." Then to Tully she explained, "Howard and George used to . . .

how do I put this?" She looked to Howard for help.

"We had some interesting friends." He took a sip of the liquor. To the senator he said, "If these old acquaintances have been coming around to me, they might be bothering George, too."

"He hasn't said anything." She caught herself and added, "But of course, he wouldn't say anything to me."

Tully rolled his eyes. She had been talking in carefully measurement phrases all day. He wasn't going to sit here and listen to them water down the details and talk around the facts.

"So you and George ran drugs," Tully said bluntly and both of them stared at him as though he had he had walked into a cocktail party naked. "Let me guess. A Columbian cartel."

Still, neither responded.

"Which means, probably cocaine, right?" Tully continued, pretending he knew the facts as he guessed.

Did they think he was stupid? The senator had been screwing with him all afternoon, doling out information ounce by ounce. That was fine until a dead guy showed up.

"No disrespect, Senator," he tamped down his impatience. "Whether you want to admit it or not, your husband is involved in something. And it looks like it's going to be messy for you politically."

She was staring at him. Her jaw clamped tight, her lipstick long gone. She had peeled out of her soaking-wet jacket but the rest of her clothing was also damp. Hair dripping and yet her hand dashed up to swipe back a disheveled strand. She didn't look any closer to budging on the truth.

Tully had never understood what he referred to as "the political class," and in the past he was grateful his dealings with them were far and few between. In Tully's opinion, they lived by an obscene creed that defied logic. A creed that raised ideologies and self-preservation above common sense.

But his new boss, Assistant Director Raymond Kunze had carved out a career by doing favors or as Tully believed – by sucking up to select congressmen and senators. Tully and Maggie had spent over a year trying to function by Kunze's ridiculous criteria.

"Are you willing to sacrifice your children for your husband?" Tully asked. This seemed to get her attention even if it looked like anger. "Are you willing to sacrifice all of them for your political career?"

"You have no right to judge me."

"Ellie," Howard said, putting a hand over hers and making it disappear but with the gentlest of touches. "Agent Tully's trying to help. And he's right. This is serious." Then he looked up at Tully. "What would you like to know?"

"You and George. What was it? Twenty-five years ago? Thirty? Florida was a major trafficking route."

"It's starting to be, again," Howard said. "A couple of the cartels are reclaiming old trafficking channels. The Sinaloa and the Zetas are warring over the routes through Juarez and Tijuana. A tremendous amount of resources have been focused on the Mexican border." Howard shrugged. "Suddenly the Gulf of Mexico and the Florida coastline are looking very good once again."

"And your old cartel?" Tully asked.

"They're calling themselves Choque Azul now. Let's just say improvisation was always one of their greatest assets. Did you see in the news, somewhere off the coast of Columbia a submarine was found?"

"Yeah, I remember reading something about that."

"The U.S. military almost immediately suspected the Russians. Maybe Chavez." Howard shook his head and smiled. "I'm pretty certain it was my old cartel. They've been looking for new vessels, new transports. Three or four months ago DEA confiscated a fishing boat off the shore of Puerto Rico. Nine hundred and twenty-five pounds of cocaine was seized. They found the bags under a boatload of mahi-

mahi. That doesn't stop them. It's big business.

"A kilo of cocaine in the highlands of Columbia or Peru is worth about two-thousand dollars. In Mexico that same kilo goes to ten-thousand. Jump the border to the US and it's suddenly worth thirty-thousand. By the time it's broken down into grams to distribute for retail, that same kilos is now one-hundred thousand dollars.

"That much money involved, it's a whole lot easier to keep finding ways to fool the DEA and the Coast Guard than to battle the Zetas and Sinaloa. The Zetas . . .? Howard stopped and studied Senator Delanor Ramos. "Well, you know from your congressional panels that it's nasty business these days."

But her eyes had wandered out to the storm. Her fingers of both hands wrapped around the glass, but Tully hadn't seen her take a sip.

"The Zetas," Howard continued. "A bunch of them got their start in this business as bodyguards for the Gulf cartels. Our bodyguards." He laughed. "They're a bunch of thugs is what they are. Years ago people got in the way they just disappeared. Used to be rumors that all the drug cartels had vats of lye. They were discreet about their kills. But this new bunch?"

He glanced at the senator again. She hadn't moved.

"They pride themselves," Howard said, "in using bloodshed to send their messages. Beheadings, dismemberment . . . anything to shock and awe not only to warn their enemies but the civilian populations in the areas where they hide in plain sight."

"Taking my family," Senator Delanor Ramos suddenly said. "Taking George and the houseboat. Do you suppose it's some sort of revenge or punishment for him not giving in to them?"

Tully wanted to ask why she thought George hadn't given in to them. But of course, he already knew why. He was her husband. However, it made perfect sense to Tully now that the situation might be quite the opposite. Not revenge. Not punishment. Was it possible that George Ramos was allowing his old drug cartel friends to use his houseboat?

He remembered the stories Howard was referring to. Tully had read about the speedboats coming into the Gulf and dumping crates and containers of drugs into the water. Then they bribed fisherman to pick them up. He hadn't thought about submarines. And actually it was a brilliant idea to use a family's houseboat. Even more brilliant in a storm like this?

The Coast Guard's response would be limited. If they did come across the houseboat their first concern would be that the family had gotten caught in the storm. A cutter would make sure they were returned safely, never suspecting that below deck there might be hundreds of pounds of cocaine stashed from a delivery in the middle of the Gulf.

That's when his cell phone finally rang. It startled him after being quiet all afternoon.

"R.J. Tully."

"Agent Tully, this is Commander Wilson." His voice sounded clipped and mechanical.

"You're back."

"Yes."

"I haven't heard from Agent O'Dell yet. How did it go?"

The Coast Guard pilot went silent.

"Commander Wilson?"

"Agent O'Dell didn't return with us."

Chapter 12

"YOUR WIFE SENT US LOOKING FOR YOU MR. RAMOS," Maggie had told the man after his son had left the steering house.

George had sent the boy back to his cabin with the promise that he would buy him his own X-box to have all to himself. Before the boy left, George said, "Just don't tell your mom." And the boy grinned like it was a familiar game. Maggie wondered how many other things the boy wasn't supposed to tell his mother.

Now he said to Maggie, "Ellie worries too much." Then to Felipe he said, "She worries about everything. What people think of her. What they say about her."

Felipe wasn't interested. Instead, he pointed to something on one of the instrument panels. Maggie couldn't see from her seat on the bench. George nodded at him and calmly said, "Probably ten to twenty minutes at the most."

"Aren't you worried at all about your children?" Liz joined in.

"You want I should shut them up?" Felipe asked.

"No, it's okay. They don't have much time left."

The way he said it made Maggie break out in a cold sweat. Her pulse started to race and she checked her wristwatch. They had ten to twenty minutes before they ended up like the crew of this houseboat.

"To answer your question, my kids grew up on boats. This . . ." He gestured out at the storm and for first time it appeared to be letting up. "This is a minor inconvenience because they can't be up on deck."

Maggie had thought – they had all believed – that George Ramos and his children had been abducted, their boat taken by force. These men certainly had a cache of serious weapons. A United States senator's husband and children would be a hefty ransom. Or it would exact a terrible blow of revenge. But George Ramos didn't look like he had his boat taken or commandeered by force. Instead, he appeared to be the one in charge.

"You're making a pickup, aren't you?" Liz asked. "Is that what this is all about?"

That drew a smile from Felipe.

"You've got it all figured out," George said but he was focused on the panel of instruments again. He clicked buttons and twisted the steering wheel. Maggie could feel the vibration as the engine revved up a notch. They were going faster. And they were turning.

"You're meeting a drug boat," Liz said, not bothering to hide her anger. "That's why you're out here in the middle of a storm." She shook her head, disgusted.

Maggie looked over at her. The woman was a rescue swimmer but as part of the Coast Guard she was a trained guardsman. Was there any way they could overpower all three men? Diego and Felipe hadn't bothered to tie their hands or restrain them. Which only told Maggie that they would not hesitate at all to shoot them if they even dared to make a wrong move.

All she could think about was that her gun was clear on the other side of boat.

"How can you do this in front of your children?" Liz asked.

This time George Ramos looked at her but he was smiling and all he said was, "Fifteen more minutes."

Maggie thought about what Liz had said. But if they were meeting a drug boat why was he speeding up? She could hear the engine hum, almost a groan as it struggled to accelerate against the choppy water. Then all of a sudden the lights flickered. Not lightning but the electrical lights, even those on the instrument panel. Another flicker and everything went black.

"What the hell?"

Maggie grabbed Liz's wrist and pulled the woman to her feet. It took no more prodding than that. Both George and Felipe exchanged curses ad Maggie and Liz were feeling their way back down the wood-paneled hallway.

Chapter 13

"WHAT DO YOU MEAN YOU LEFT AGENT O'DELL on the houseboat? How the hell did she get from your helicopter down onto the houseboat?"

"Oh, my God. They found the boat," Senator Delanor Ramos said when she overheard him. "Where are they? Are they okay?"

He waved her off. He was having a difficult enough time trying to hear what Wilson was telling him.

"A cutter is on its way," the commander explained. "We couldn't stay in the air or we'd be knocked out of the sky."

"You still didn't tell me how Agent O'Dell ended up on the boat."

"She left the helicopter without my consent. She disregarded my order."

Okay, Tully thought, so that did sound like Maggie, but only if she believed something serious was going down.

"What exactly do you think happened to the boat?"

"We couldn't see anyone on board. But RS Bailey was giving us mixed signals."

"What about George and the kids? Are they okay?" The senator grew impatient.

"Hold on, Commander," Tully said and to the senator,

"They couldn't see anyone on board. A cutter's on its way."

"Oh, my God." Her fingers were back to twisting her wedding ring.

"Commander, won't it take forever in this storm for a cutter to find the houseboat?"

"They've been tracking it on radar ever since we gave them its position. Their turbo engines should put them on location any time now."

"Listen," Tully said, trying to figure out if anything he could tell the Coast Guard would even make a difference. "We have reason to believe members of a drug cartel took over the boat."

"Wait a minute, how do you know that? We haven't received anything."

Tully ignored the senator's pained look. "I have nothing official, okay? But you need to warn that cutter. There are most likely armed men aboard."

Chapter 14

MAGGIE THOUGHT SHE COULD HEAR ANOTHER NOISE. Not a helicopter but a loud hum approaching. If Liz was right about them picking up a drug delivery then there was another boat close by. Right now all she could think about was getting through the pitch-black hallway. Liz stayed quiet. She kept her hand on Maggie's shoulder and followed. She knew exactly where Maggie was headed.

They could already hear Felipe stumbling to find them back in the steering house. George wouldn't be able to leave as long as the boat's engine was engaged. Though she didn't know that for sure. Boat's probably had auto-pilot but could it be used in a storm?

Felipe was yelling to Diego in Spanish. And for a second Maggie worried that they might run right into the man. Had he finished flinging the dead crewmembers over the railing? Or was he back here in the laundry room retrieving the last one?

She held her breath, trying to listen. But she didn't slow down her pace. The engine still chugged and vibrated the floorboards. Certainly Diego would be cursing in the dark if he had been in the laundry room or even the hallway when the lights went out.

Her hip ran into a kitchen counter. She bit down on her lip but felt relief more than pain. If they'd made it to the kitchen they had passed the laundry room. The only window was farther down, past the living room, past another hallway of floor to ceiling cherry wood paneling and bookcases. Not that windows mattered. It was too dark. Still, Maggie could see a flicker of lightning at the end of the tunnel.

"Two more doors," Liz whispered and Maggie realized that the rescue swimmer had counted them when they had been hostages.

At the other end of the hallway behind them she could hear Felipe slamming through the door from the steering house. It wouldn't take him any time at all to make his way through in the dark. Everything was bolted down. Maggie couldn't even shove anything in his path to slow him down.

Then the engine sputtered and went silent. George had turned it off. And now there were three men to worry about.

"Just on the other side of the next bookcase," Liz whispered again.

Maggie grabbed Liz's arm and exchanged places with her. If she had to, she knew she could take down Felipe, especially if he didn't see it coming. As if reading her mind, Liz kept hold of Maggie's wrist and pulled her along.

"It's right here," she said and the two of them patted down the wall looking for the door latch.

Liz found it first. The blast of wind and rain hit them in the face like buckshot. Maggie had to hold her breath. She tucked her chin and grab onto the railing. The tackle box would be close and yet Maggie couldn't see a foot in front of her.

Then she realized Liz was down on her hands and knees. She joined her.

"It's not here," Liz yelled.

"It has to be."

Lightning flashed and Maggie saw the box clamped down. She crawled closer. She could see the bungee cord that cinched the lid. A wave washed over the deck railing, knocking both of them into the wall. Maggie swiped a hand over her face and through the blur she thought she saw a light on the water. She pointed for Liz.

"Drug boat?"

Liz shook her head. "Bigger. I think it might be the cutter."

It was close. Minutes away. And yet, Maggie knew they might be dead in minutes.

She reached for the bungee cord and suddenly the deck lit up. A big man with a spotlight stood at the other end. Diego. He stood almost exactly in the same place where she had seen him with the RPG. This time he had the spotlight in one hand and an automatic rifle in the other.

Maggie continued to slide closer to the tackle box. Diego was shouting at them in Spanish. She grabbed the bungee cord and worked her hand under the lid. The box was deep. Where it had taken no time to toss her weapon down into it, it would take reaching her entire arm to find it. Before her fingers made purchase Felipe stormed out the same door.

He was angry. He was screaming at them but pointing and gesturing to Diego about the light that was approaching. Only now did Maggie realize that Liz had positioned herself, once again, in front of Maggie so that the men couldn't see. Maggie continued to slide her hand to the other side of the tackle box. Her arm was behind her and Felipe hadn't noticed quite yet. He still didn't suspect that they would have access to weapons. He thought they only wanted to escape.

Felipe gestured now for Diego to hurry while he waved the automatic handgun in Liz and Maggie's faces. He was speaking too quickly for Maggie to understand but she knew they would need to move Maggie and Liz to the other side of the boat, away from the approaching light so they could shoot them and throw them overboard.

Why couldn't she find her gun?

That's when George Ramos came out the door. He stood

between them – Diego and Felipe on one side, legs spread and balancing themselves like experts in the wind and rain. On the other side was Liz and Maggie still on their knees. George looked to Maggie and held something up, waving it around above his head. In the glare of the spotlight she thought it looked like a gun.

"Is this what you're looking for, Agent O'Dell?"

Her service revolver. And she felt her stomach drop.

George Ramos brought the gun down. His arm stretched out. He fired two shots, expertly hitting both of his targets. The first caught Diego between the eyes. The second blast slammed into Felipe's right temple.

Chapter 15

THE RAIN HAD LET UP. EVEN THE WIND appeared to be giving them a break. But Tully saw lightning brighten the horizon just over the water. It would indeed be only a break. There was definitely more to come.

Moments ago the cutter had arrived with the houseboat named Electric Blue in tow. No one was allowed to board until given permission. Senator Delanor Ramos was not pleased but she waited.

When he saw Maggie he hardly recognized her. She still wore the orange flight suit. Her hair was a tangled mess. Her skin almost a sickly white. She and Liz Bailey stood shoulder to shoulder as the Coast Guard brass made them go through their ridiculous protocol.

Very little had been relayed back to them on shore, but they were told that George Ramos and his two children were safe and unharmed. Two men had, indeed, boarded the houseboat and attempted to take it over. Three members of Ramos's crew had been killed. And from what Tully understood, the two gunmen were also dead.

"I knew George would never put our children in danger," Senator Delanor Ramos said as she stood beside Tully.

They watched from inside the air station. Tully glanced

over at her. Her tote bag in his rental SUV had provided her with a change of clothing. She had reapplied makeup and fixed her hair. The façade was back in place, everything back to normal. For her sake and for her kids, he hoped that was the case. After listening to Howard about drug cartels reclaiming old routes Tully didn't believe that this story was that easily explained away. If it were, George's "business associate," Ricardo wouldn't be dead. Tully was anxious to hear George's explanation.

****

On the pier, Maggie watched Liz. She was better at this than Maggie was. There would be reports to file and statements to sign. The Coast Guard and Homeland Security would make sure everything was properly handled. And at the same time, Maggie wanted to take Liz aside and ask, "What the hell happened out there?"

The cutter had taken on the houseboat within minutes of George Ramos shooting Diego and Felipe. When he pulled Maggie and Liz inside from the bloody deck he told them how relieved he was. That he had been frightened for his children. He handed them towels from the closest bathroom and offered them brandy. And the whole time Maggie noticed that he hadn't put down her revolver. He kept it in his hand like a reminder that he was still in charge. And it was in his hand when he stepped back out onto the lower deck, leaving them inside the cozy living room with the generator partially restoring electricity.

Maggie shouldn't have been surprised when George Ramos explained his story to the Coast Guard crew. Both she and Liz agreed that they didn't know what the situation was before they boarded. Drained and exhausted, Maggie realized that some things were not as they appeared. It wasn't impossible that a father would pretend to go along with a couple of madmen if he knew it would save his children.

George claimed the men had threatened him and were forcing him to meet their drug connection somewhere in the Gulf of Mexico. That scenario wasn't far from what Liz had suspected. He made his story sound so convincing that even Maggie found herself backtracking. She tried to remember pieces of dialogue. She still couldn't figure out how and when he had managed to get her gun out of the tackle box. Why had she been so sure that George was not only friends with Diego and Felipe, but that he was the one in charge?

"A man does whatever he needs to do to protect his children," George Ramos kept saying and twice he had said it while looking directly at Maggie and Liz.

Maggie wondered if the children would ever be questioned. She doubted it. Though she realized the children probably didn't know anything more than what their father had told them. They had been stashed away in their bedrooms playing video games.

As they exited the cutter she watched George with Angelica and Daniel as they met Senator Delanor Ramos on the pier. George scooped up Daniel and the family huddled together, exchanging hugs and kisses.

"It's the damned thing," Liz said, walking alongside Maggie.

Now that they were finally alone Maggie stopped and waited for Liz's eyes. It was breezy out in the middle of the pier but the rain was light and actually felt good. Behind them, crews were securing the cutter and the houseboat.

"Do you believe him?" she asked.

Liz glanced around. She nodded at someone and Maggie turned to see Tully making his way to them. Before Tully was in earshot, Liz answered, "Not in a million years."

"You're a sight for sore eyes," Tully said and surprised Maggie with a bear hug.

He patted Liz on the shoulder as she left them to rejoin her aircrew who were already yelling catcalls at her from the end of the pier.

"You okay?" he asked as they walked and followed in Liz's direction.

"I think I'll leave the helicopter rides to you in the future."

"That's a deal."

They were almost to the parking lot when Maggie noticed George Ramos heading back down the pier to his houseboat.

"What's he doing?" she asked Tully.

"Maybe he wants to get it to the marina and into its slip before the next bands of weather. It's an expensive boat."

She saw Senator Delanor Ramos and the two children getting into a black Escalade. Tully was probably right.

"Lots of holes in his story," Tully said as if reading her mind. "I doubt he's going to be asked to fill in any of those."

"Does his wife believe him?"

"I think she has to."

"Maybe I can ask him just one last question," Maggie said. She glanced over at Tully. "Care to come along?"

"I wouldn't miss it."

"Let the poor man board his boat first," she told him and they took up a leisurely pace.

George Ramos waved to the cutter's crew as he passed them on the pier. They were leaving as he went back to his boat. It had been a hell of night. Maggie could hear the men wishing him well. He didn't even notice Tully and Maggie as he climbed onto the lower deck of Electric Blue. He didn't look back as he entered the same side door where he had shot Diego and Felipe. All the blood had been washed away by the waves and the rain. The cutter crew hadn't been at all surprised when George explained how both men had fallen overboard when he shot them with her revolver.

But Liz and Maggie knew that the men hadn't fallen overboard. George had gone back out before the cutter arrived.

Maggie suspected he was lying about much more. Everyone presumed that the houseboat hadn't met up with the drug boat yet. That they were headed to pick up the delivery when Liz and Maggie interrupted. But what if they were wrong? What if they were on their way back?

Maggie gestured for Tully to climb aboard behind her. She opened the door gently, quietly and before she went inside she saw Tully had his weapon drawn. Hers was still being held by the Coast Guard.

With the dim lights, it was easy to follow the narrow hallway. She could hear George in one of the bedrooms down passed the kitchen. It sounded like he was moving furniture but Maggie knew that wasn't possible. Everything was bolted down. Before she got to the open bedroom door, she pressed her back against the paneled hallway wall and let Tully go around her.

She stayed in place and watched him step into the doorway. She watched Tully's face and immediately she knew that she was right.

Tully aimed his weapon and cleared his throat. "Stay right where you are, Mr. Ramos."

When Maggie looked in she couldn't believe it. The storage bins were pulled out from under the bed. A window bench was open exposing another storage area. All of them were stacked and packed with bags of cocaine.

George Ramos smiled and shook his head like he couldn't believe it.

"This is not what it looks like," he said.

"Choque Azul," Tully said suddenly. "I can't believe I missed it but my Spanish isn't so great." He glanced at Maggie but kept his Glock pointed on Ramos. "The drug cartel George used to work for. They call themselves Choque Azul now. Doesn't that mean Blue Shock?" Then to Ramos, he said, "You named your boat after them."

"Electric Blue," Maggie said. "This wasn't your first drug run."

"I can explain this." Ramos actually looked worried now.

"But we'll make sure it's your last," she added.

NEW YORK TIMES BESTSELLING AUTHORS
J.T. ELLISON
WHITEOUT
WASHINGTON, D.C.

Epigraph

"The wise man in the storm prays to God, not for safety from danger, but deliverance from fear."

— Ralph Waldo Emerson

Chapter 1

October 9, 1987
Annecy, France
1900 Hours

My father's screams echo in the small car.

"Monte, vite, vite. Angelie, baisse-toi! Baisse-toi!"

My head hits the floor just as the window shatters. Blood, thick and hot, sprays my bare legs. I wedge myself under my mother's skirts, her thighs heavy against my shoulders. Somehow I know she is already dead. We are all dead.

Flashes of black.

Their voices, two distinctly male, one female. Another, a stranger's call, silenced abruptly with a short fusillade of bullets. The would-be savior's bicycle smashes into the side of our aging Peugeot. His body catapults across the hood onto the pavement beyond and his head hits the ground; the crack sounds like the opening of a cantaloupe, ripe and hard.

My father, his life leaving him, slides down in the seat like a puppet cut from its strings. He's whispering words over and over, faintly, and with the cacophony in the background I can barely hear him. I risk a glance, wishing I'd not. The image shall never leave me. Red, pulpy and viscous. He is missing half his face, but his full lips are moving.

"Si toi survivre, cherchér ton Oncle Pierre. Je t'aime de tout mon cœur."

I hear nothing but the first words. Panic fills me. Though

I recognize what is happening, the reality has just crept in.

Si toi survivre. If you survive.

I want to take his hand, to comfort him, to tell him I am there, that I, too, love him with all my heart. I reach for him as he dies. He shakes his head, trying to implore me to stay hidden, not to move. He isn't even speaking now, but I can hear his words in my head, like he has transferred his soul to my body for these last fluttering moments, has given himself up early to crowd into my body and try to save me.

Undeterred, my hand steals across the gearshift. I touch the cold skin of his thumb.

A roaring in my ears. There is pain beyond anything I've ever felt, and I go blank.

Chapter 2

October 8, 2013
Nashville, Tennessee
0415 Hours

Homicide never sleeps. At least that's what Taylor Jackson told herself when the phone rousted her from a moderately deep slumber, the first decent shut-eye she'd had in a week. She'd finally crashed at 3:00 a.m., succumbing to the two-to-three hours she normally managed on a good night. The sheets were tangled around her legs, so she rolled to Baldwin's side of the bed, used a long arm to snake the phone off the hook.

"Who, what, where, when, and, most importantly, why?"

Homicide detective Lincoln Ross didn't miss a beat.

"Me. Your wake up call. Your phone. 4:15 a.m. Because you told me to get you up so you didn't miss your flight."

"You're fired."

"Excellent. I'll charter a plane to the Bahamas right now. See ya."

She yawned. "Okay, okay. I'm up. You downstairs?"

A faint horn sounded.

"On my way."

At least no one was dead. Not yet, anyway.

Jeans, boots, black cashmere T-shirt, leather jacket, ponytail, Carmex. Three minutes flat. Take that, Heidi Klum.

Two hours and three Diet Cokes later, her somewhat

caffeinated body in an exit row window seat, the 737 rushed into the sky. She watched the ground fall away and asked herself again why she'd agreed to do this. The invitation had been the fault—*now, Taylor, be nice*—the *inspiration* of her fiancé, John Baldwin, whose place she was taking at the Freedom Conference, a small foreign intelligence initiative that met annually to hear about the latest tools for cyber intelligence and information gathering. The professional makeup of the conference was specific to clandestine services, but some civilian law enforcement officials attended as well. Baldwin had been set to speak about using behavioral profiling as a predictive analysis for terrorist attacks against the United States, and was featuring the case of the Pretender, a nasty serial killer who'd killed dozens in his bid to ruin all of their lives.

To ruin her life, as well.

Two years in the past, the moniker conjured chills and made her throat tighten.

Dead. He's dead. Stop it.

Baldwin had been called off at the last minute to deal with a skinner in Montana—what was it about these freaks who liked to remove their victims' skin?—and Taylor had agreed to take his place at the conference. She had his notes, his slideshow, though she was thinking of skipping that—there were crime scene photos from Nashville that showed her own bloodstains, and pools of her best friend's blood. She didn't know if she was quite ready to see them at all, not to mention plastered, bigger than life, on a presentation screen for an entire audience to see.

It had been interesting to see his analytical write-up about the case. It was so cut and dried. Like there were no other options. In Baldwin's world, everything that transpired was a foregone conclusion based on several psychological metrics. His evaluation made her feel better about what had happened. Taylor had lost her head. She'd hunted the man down, gone off grid in order to kill him, nearly lost her own life in the process, but in the end, it was Baldwin's finger that pulled the trigger.

He'd done that for her.

A foregone conclusion.

She settled deeper into the seat, shut her eyes. The least she could do was give his speech for him.

Chapter 3

October 7, 2013
London, England
0000 Hours

The phone in my flat bleats to life as I am leaving for the airport.

My phone never rings, and this is purposeful. It is there for emergencies: fires, break-ins, unanticipated scenarios that could lead to my death. It is not for casual conversations, and it never rings, because only one person has my number.

My heart speeds up, just a little. *Why is he calling? Why now?*

I pick up the receiver. "*Oui*?"

"Angelie. What have you done?"

"*Je ne sais pas de quoi tu parles.*"

"In English, Angelie. How many times have I told you?"

"*Alors*, Pierre. Fine. I don't know what you're talking about."

"Angelie, you know exactly what I'm talking about. A couple of *gendârmes* just pulled Gregoire Campion's body out of a duffel bag that was stashed in his bathtub. He was in pieces."

This news is both good and bad. Good, because the smug bastard is dead, at last. Bad, because if my Uncle Pierre is telling the truth and the body has been found so soon, the borders will be under extra scrutiny. Pierre has given me a gift without even knowing.

"That means nothing to me. I must go, *Oncle. À bientôt.*"

I hear his cry of protest as I drop the receiver. I must hurry.

From my closet I pull the necessary gear. A quick change of undergarments gives my thin body curves; tinted contacts turn my eyes blue; a beautifully made wig transforms me into an elegant blonde. I trade my jeans and trainers for a cashmere dress that clings perfectly to every inch of my altered body. A pair of knee-high leather Frye boots with specially made lifts adds a good three inches to my five-foot-four frame.

My name is now Alana Terbraak. I have been this woman before. Alana is fearless, a predator disguised as a Dutch-Canadian travel agent. She is the perfect cover for crossing borders; it is her job to scope out areas she sends her clients to. No one questions Alana's travel. She is one of my better identities.

I place several remaining identities in the bag, under a secure flap that is impossible to see with the naked eye, and pull the worn Canadian dollars from my safe. I mix them in with my Euros and pound notes, wipe down the small flat, lock everything up, and leave.

My plane departs in two hours, and I will not miss it.

Chapter 4

October 8, 2013
Washington, D.C.
1400 Hours

An early snow greeted Taylor when she landed in D.C. As promised, a man was waiting for her by Baggage, holding an iPad; the screen spelled out her name. He took her bag silently and led her to a black sedan. Flakes danced around her, floating generously from an icy sky. She was glad for the warmth of the car.

When they were on the road, he offered her a drink. "There's bottled water, Scotch, and vodka in that cooler by your feet."

"Thank you." Taylor took a water. It was too early to drink, even though it might warm her from the inside out.

The snow continued to cascade down as they drove to the west, getting heavier the closer they got to the Chesapeake Bay. Charles, the driver, slowed, taking it easy; the roads were getting slick.

Taylor gave up, turned up the heat in the backseat. "Too bad you don't have hot chocolate in here. I didn't know snow was in the forecast."

"It wasn't. We've got an Alberta Clipper that snuck up on us, same storm that's wreaking havoc back in the Midwest and down in Florida. It's a good thing you flew in today. Tomorrow you'd be stuck at the airport, shivering your skinny self off. Gonna get bad, that's what they're saying. Big blizzard, storm surge up the bay, power lines down from the ice. Hope you brought a sweater."

"I did. My friend Maggie O'Dell—she's an FBI agent—called last night and warned me that the storm was going to be bad. When Maggie speaks, I listen."

Forty minutes and several white-knuckled slips and slides later, Charles deposited her at the front steps of the Old Maryland Resort and Spa. "I'll bring up your bag. You're to meet the conference folk at the desk."

"Thanks, Charles. And thanks for getting me here in one piece." Taylor tried to hand him a tip, but he brushed it off with a shy smile. She shivered in her leather jacket and mounted the stairs to the resort's reception area. A woman waved at her the moment she walked in the door. She was small to the point of being elfin, gray hair cut into a chic chin-length bob, cornflower blue eyes, and a friendly smile. Taylor felt a bit like a linebacker on her approach.

"Welcome to Maryland, Lieutenant Jackson. I'm Cherry Gregg, the chair of the Freedom Conference. We are so glad to have you here. Was the ride from the airport okay?"

"It was great, thank you. I appreciate you sending a car for me." That was a lie; Taylor had wanted to rent a car, not liking the idea of being stuck an hour out of D.C. on the Chesapeake Bay without her own transportation, but it was all part of the speaker gig—getting coddled and treated like royalty. Samantha Owens, her best friend, lived in Georgetown, and was planning to come down at the end of the weekend and ferry Taylor back to D.C. for a night of catch-up. She could live for two days without a car, especially because the conference was being held at a lavish spa resort that seemed to have every amenity she might need.

"If you're anything like me, you hate not having your own car, but we are at your service this weekend. Anyplace you'd like to go, just call down to the desk, and your driver will ferry you about like a queen."

Taylor didn't even bother trying to hide her surprise. "You read my mind. How did you know?"

Gregg answered with a slight laugh. "Lieutenant, I was a CIA field agent for twenty years, and COS—sorry, Chief of Station—in four different countries. Reliable transportation was always my number-one priority. If you get completely desperate, there's an Enterprise car rental four blocks south."

Taylor laughed, liking Gregg immediately. "I'll remember that. Is the weather going to hold up?"

"It's not. Thankfully, you're the last one to arrive. We've got everyone else safely here already. We're told they have back up generators and enough fuel to hold us for at least a week, should we be so unlucky as to lose power, and the kitchens are fully stocked. There are fireplaces in many of the rooms with plenty of wood, too. One of the treats of this place, and it's going to work in our favor this weekend."

"Sounds like they thought of everything."

"Oh, they did, I assure you. Most importantly, the bar is prepped and ready, too. They laid in an extra ration of grog for us all."

"Priorities. I like it."

"You bet. I'm so happy you could join us, Lieutenant. You're very kind to take over Dr. Baldwin's spot. Would you like to settle into your room, then meet me back here in two hours? We've got a cocktail reception we'd like you to attend—it's business dress. We'll get you introduced to the other panelists, and there's a fair amount of people who'd like to meet you. Your story, your history . . . well, let's just say folks are interested."

Folks were always interested. Taylor attracted trouble like dust on black furniture. Inevitable.

"I don't know if that's good or bad, but you're too kind. Thank you."

"Here's your key—you're up on the fifth floor, in the Maryland Suite. I've been told they used to call it the Crab Cake Suite, but people complained."

They shared another laugh, and Taylor set off for the elevators. The room was at the end of a long, narrow hallway.

She held her pass to the door, and it unlocked.

Her first impression was a blizzard of white—white walls, white furniture, white bedding, white carpeting. The cleaning bills must be astronomical. There was a fireplace at the far end of the suite, and the bathroom walls were clear glass, with a hot tub that had a perfect view of the fire.

She started to giggle, took a picture and texted it, then dialed Baldwin's cell. He answered on the first ring.

"I would suggest you plan to drink champagne instead of red wine."

"I know, right? The picture doesn't do it justice." She went to the windows, pulled back the heavy curtains. "Baldwin, you should see this place. The view of the Chesapeake Bay is spectacular, or would be in the summer—right now it's just snowing. But you saw that hot tub and fireplace. It's like the sex bomb suite or something."

"Sounds more like a honeymoon suite. I'm sorry I have to miss it." There was a note in his voice that made her stomach hitch.

"I'm sorry too. Though I am wondering why, exactly, they reserved this particular room for *you.*"

"I'd told them you were coming," he replied.

She started to laugh then, and he joined her.

"You're naughty. Everything moving along with your skinner?"

"Don't tell anyone, but we're serving a warrant in an hour. I think we've nailed the psycho."

"That's my guy. Always gets his man. Good job."

"Thanks, hon. Just glad to get another monster off the streets. Listen, there's a really bad storm heading your way. So stay inside, stay warm and dry, and if you get stuck there, I'll come and rescue you. And we can see what the real view is from that hot tub. Okay?"

"Sounds wonderful. Love you. Bye."

She unpacked her suitcase. Business casual for the cocktail party—she guessed jeans wouldn't work. She pulled a black wool skirt from the bag, and switched her motorcycle boots for knee-high cognac leather. A black cashmere sweater set and her grandmother's pearls completed the outfit. She glanced in the mirror.

"You look entirely too respectable." She took her hair down, let it hang loose around her shoulders.

"Better. Much less uptight."

And the woman in the mirror grinned back.

Chapter 5

Chesapeake Bay, Maryland
1700 Hours

Taylor allowed herself a second glass of wine. The cocktail party was in full swing, the stories flying fast and furious. After the initial round of introductions, and a few awkward questions answered blithely, she'd stuck to listening, watching. There was a beautiful brunette built like a brick shithouse across the way who'd garnered the attention of practically every man in the place. She had a wonderfully exotic accent, a loud voice, and was telling stories about Sudan's second civil war in the '80s. Something about Gaddafi switching sides to support Mengistu, and a microfiche that she'd planted to thwart a southern attack.

" . . . But he never thought to look in the lid of the teapot, and believe you me, I've never looked at cinnamon tea the same way again," and the crowd roared with appreciative laughter.

Taylor smiled to herself and crossed the room to watch the storm. Snow on water fascinated her. Nashville wasn't a bastion of winter weather; it just got cold, and rarely snowed more than an inch or two. This was a full-fledged blizzard, and it was monstrously beautiful.

"Intelligence officers. We're like bees: we can only speak in one language, and if you don't know it, there's no manual for translation."

Taylor turned to see the man who'd spoken. He was in his late fifties, small and dapper, with short gray hair and a sad smile, and the barest hint of an accent. French, she thought, though it was very refined.

"Oh, we cops are the same way. Our stories are usually bloodier, though."

"Give them time. A few more pops, and they'll be into Afghanistan. Plenty of bloody stories there. I'm Thierry Florian. I know your fiancé. He's a good man. We worked together in Argentina last year."

"Ah, Argentina. So that's where he was. I knew it was South America, but Baldwin is always very careful not to disclose too much of his . . . private work."

"Nature of the beast. Helps to have a spouse in the business. No awkward questions at two in the morning."

"We're not married. Yet."

"There's time." His head was cocked to the side like a spaniel. "Your photos don't do you justice. Your eyes are different colors. Your right is darker than your left. I've never seen heterochromia with gray like that. *C'est trés jolie*. Very pretty."

He wasn't hitting on her, just noticing. It still felt weird, so she changed the subject. "Are you still clandestine service then, Thierry?"

"I retired from the DGSE in November after thirty years in. I run the Macallan Group now. Do you know who we are?"

"I know you're not a bunch of Scotch enthusiasts."

He laughed. "That's right. We grew out of the Futures Working Group, but we are a privately held company. Very dedicated, and very much off book." He winked.

"Baldwin's told me about your work. You've assembled an interesting gang of people."

"We have people from every section, multiple countries. From CIA to Mossad and military to police. We even have a couple of novelists, brilliant men and women whose sole purpose is to dream up the most unfathomable situations for us to scrutinize, because real life always imitates art."

"Doesn't it though."

His shoulders shrugged, a perfectly Gallic gesture Taylor had never seen an American man master. "*Oui*. It is strange, life. Any time you want to join us, say the word. You have just the right temperament to fit in. I was hoping to discuss it with you this weekend."

Taylor raised her eyebrows. "What, you want me to come to a meeting or something?"

She envisioned pipes and dark smoky rooms, green computer screens and cables spitting out from teletype machines. Romantic thoughts of spies long past—which was silly, because she'd seen Baldwin at work, and it wasn't cool and dreamy. It was brutal, and watching him in that element always gave her a chill down the spine. When he shut down his compassion, his became another person entirely.

Florian gave a small laugh. "So to speak. The meeting in question would be of a more permanent nature."

"Oh. Are you offering me a job?"

"I am. I would like to hook Baldwin, too. He understands our mission, that our work is vital to the safety of all of our countries. Like the intelligence services, we collect and analyze data, only act when necessary. We share with many of them if we see they are behind the curve ball."

Act when necessary. Again, she was getting into a shadow world she didn't like to think of. Some would see it as breaking the law, something she was vehemently opposed to. But for the greater good, as Baldwin always liked to point out—for the greater good, rules were sometimes meant to be bent and broken. And if it saved lives? Absolutely.

"I think you mean behind the eight ball."

"*Alors*, my English. Yes. The eight ball. But more importantly, we use the information we collect to anticipate. Anticipate, and avoid. The problem with the FBI, with your police forces, with law enforcement, in general, is the very nature of the work. React, react, react. The CIA is better, but even they are stymied by their political ties. Black ops hardly exist anymore. There is no funding for special programs, and no balls on your politicians.

"Our work is entirely independent and very proactive. We want to prevent the attacks before they start, rather than hunt down the perpetrators after the fact. You talk John Baldwin into coming along, and you can name your price. You are both worth it."

"That's very kind, but it's not about the money—"

"Of course not. You are, I believe the right word is, an idealist. You fight for justice, because ever fiber of your being screams that it is the right thing to do. Just think, Taylor Jackson, what power there would be in *preventing* the attacks you investigate, *before* they occur. That is our job. And your unique abilities are worth a great deal to me.

"You both come from money; you have also earned enough to retire comfortably. So think of this salary as a cushion. You can buy his-and-hers Ferraris, or give it away to starving African children, I do not care. I need your minds. You are instinctive, and smart, and you could do a lot of good for your country. Think about it. *Santé.*"

He clinked her glass and walked away.

She took a sip of wine to cover her discomfiture. *Well. That was interesting.*

She dismissed the conversation. She was perfectly happy working homicide for Metro Nashville. She didn't like change. She especially didn't like the idea of abandoning her team.

And preventing murder? Preventing attacks? No one could do that, not effectively. Someone evil would always slip through the cracks.

The snow was heavier than ever, coming down so hard she could barely see the lights of the cars passing by on the street below. She checked her phone; the forecast was now calling for twenty inches. A small bloom of panic started in her chest. The last time she'd been snowed in, a blizzard of epic proportions in Scotland, not-so-great things had happened.

Florian caught her eye from across the room and smiled politely. He was clearly watching her, and she resented it, though she didn't know why. He'd made an offer. She'd gotten them before. It was what it was.

But. . . .

She'd be forty in a few years, and as far as her career was concerned, she would need to make a decision about her role going forward. It was already being whispered that she'd make Captain soon, would be in charge of Nashville's entire Criminal Investigative Division, and that meant she'd be off the streets and on to the paperwork and political glad-handing. Captain Jackson. A few more years, then further up the brass ladder. Maybe even Chief in ten years. More bureaucratic nonsense. And then what? Run for office? No, thank you. She had too many opinions and not enough reserve to stop her from sharing them freely.

Baldwin wanted her to join the FBI, which would be a logical step. And though she admired everything he did, she knew she wouldn't fit in. The culture was too restrictive. She had enough bossing around at Metro that drove her mad. Having to follow the kind of dictates that the federal government imposed on law enforcement was a recipe for disaster.

The Macallan Group. Proactive rather than reactive. Huh.

She looked around the room again for Thierry Florian, but didn't see him. She sent him a mental *thanks a lot*. There would be no sleep for her tonight.

Chapter 6

October 9
Chesapeake Bay, Maryland
0000 Hours

The cameras are on for my safety. I made sure before we began. They will catch everything. Just in case.

The kisses are going a mile a minute. Our clothes are gone, my slip is rucked up over my hips. I skipped panties, hopeful for this moment. It makes things so much easier. His hands rush over my body, grasping my skin, kneading my buttocks, hands hurrying to my thighs and then my back, up and down and around, and I whisper, "Too fast, too fast."

He slows, smiling, his right palm lingering along the curve of my hip, then sliding to my breast, his mouth featherweight, following his touch.

Better.

It has been too long. I should stop him before it goes much further, but it feels so good to be touched, to be loved.

His hand slips down between my thighs, and a moan escapes my lips. *Stay in control, stay in control,* but I am losing it. He is too good, too skilled, and I hit the point where I don't care anymore. I am just an animal, needing, wanting. His finger is deep inside me, and we are still standing, skin-to-skin, glued together. And it feels so good.

Fuck it. I inch up, and he catches the movement, effortlessly lifts me, and my legs wrap around his waist. He is breathing hard, ready to go. Pushing against me. Waves of pleasure shudder through me. I think I might faint, take a deep breath to clear my head.

He catches my lips, kissing, sucking, staring into my eyes. He moves his hand, and I can't help but respond.

Recognizing it is time, he lays me down on the bed and slows his movement further, stroking, caressing, gentling when I want it rough, the mistake of a new lover. "Now," I urge, and he smiles and spreads my legs wide, one palm on the inside of each thigh, and thrusts into me, hard. I cry out, go right over the edge into the bliss, and he comes with me.

I lose time; I always do after sex. Hazardous, but inescapable. Hence the cameras. An old habit, hard to break.

When our breathing slows, he rolls off me, to the side, and I rise from the bed.

"Don't get up," he says, leaning on an elbow, beckoning me back.

Too late. I am already at my purse, the bag open, the cold steel in my hand. My favorite companion, the only one I truly trust. I turn to him, a brief smile playing on my lips.

"Thank you," I say, and fire. The suppressed round sounds like a sigh in the darkened room. It takes him between the eyes, and he collapses back onto the bed.

Another means to an end.

I replace the weapon, dress, brush my hair, enjoy the flush of color on my cheeks. I wipe down the room, grab my cell phone, turn off the video camera. Face the connecting door to the room next to my newly dead lover.

A moment twenty-five years in the making. Finally here.

I jimmy the lock, silent as possible. The door opens, and there he is. Asleep, quiet. Far from innocent. He looks older in his sleep.

Older, and soon to be very, very dead.

Chapter 7

0110 Hours

Taylor showered and changed, then stalked around her suite, wishing for something to do. No pool table, as the bar was closed for the night. Baldwin was getting some well-earned sleep, having made a successful arrest. She'd forgotten to pack a book, though there was probably a library on the hotel grounds.

Truth be told, nothing would distract her enough. She was worried about the storm. The gathering winds were howling past her window; a small piece of siding had come loose and was rattling. She could just make out people moving around outside—workers, most likely, sent out into the storm to batten down the hatches. They worked in twos, probably tied together so they wouldn't get lost.

A scene from a Laura Ingalls Wilder book pranced into her head, something she'd not thought about since she was a child. The rope between the shed and the house, followed to feed the animals, so Pa wouldn't get lost. Or Laura. She couldn't remember exactly who was meant to be saved by the slender thread, but it had worked, and all ended well.

She had no tether to keep her safe, and it worried her.

The television gave no succor, either. The whole country seemed to be in the grip of this massive and mercurial storm. The Weather Channel was covering the huge, multi-state event causing chaos across the country. The mega-storm had swooped down from Canada, slicing through Illinois, where Rockford had received record-breaking snow totals, and people were still lost, stuck on highways and in houses inaccessible to rescue crews. She sent her friend Mary Catherine Riggio a text, checking on her, knowing the Rockford P.D. homicide detective would be out helping the emergency prep folks, but didn't hear back. And poor Maggie was down in Pensacola, Florida, which was flooded out after twenty inches of rain, and still experiencing thunderstorms and high winds. Major damage. The radar clearly showed the catastrophic storm heading right toward the Washington, D.C., area, which meant Taylor was now directly in its path.

The Weather Channel's anchor warned everyone to hunker down, because it was going to get worse before it got better. The snow totals were going to break records all up the Eastern seaboard, the storm surges would cause widespread flooding up and down the Chesapeake Bay.

Great.

As a first responder herself, Taylor wasn't used to sitting in a hotel room waiting for a storm to hit. If this were Nashville, she'd be in the command center at Metro, giving instructions, helping the city cover all the quadrants to minimize the danger to its citizens. She gave a moment's thought to calling the Calvert County Sheriff, offering her services, but realized she'd be as wanted as a wart.

She lit the fire, grabbed a beer from the mini-fridge, snuggled into the bed, and watched the flames dance while she listened to the warnings. When she could take no more, she flipped off The Weather Channel, found *The Princess Bride* on one of the movie channels, and turned down the lights. She knew the words practically by heart, but it was better than nothing.

The R.O.U.S., Rodents of Unusual Size, were beginning to lurk when the power went off.

The fireplace was down to coals as well. She'd burned through more logs than she'd realized, and the stash was getting low.

Taylor picked up the room phone, heard nothing. She pressed a few buttons, but no dial tone started. Thankfully, she'd thought to charge her cell phone. She called down to the front desk. Nothing. The lines were dead.

She knew the hotel had generators, she just needed them to kick in. It would get cold in the room quickly—the fireplace didn't put off that much heat—so she grabbed the extra blanket from the armoire and tossed it on the end of the bed.

Nothing to do but wait, and try to sleep. After an hour of tossing and turning, she managed to drift, her rest disturbed by terrible dreams. She was cold, so cold, hiking through the snow, with no one in sight, just the expanse of white spreading in all directions. She knew it was the end; she wouldn't survive. And the voice of the Pretender whispered in her ear.

Chapter 8

0200 Hours

It was two in the morning when the fire alarms went off. She scrambled from the bed, shaking off the chill, not sure if it was the temperature or the dreams, and threw on her jeans. It was cold in the room, her fingers fumbled with the buttons. After shrugging into her jacket, she pocketed her cell and wallet, and opened the door to the hallway with care. She could smell smoke.

Other guests were streaming from their rooms. Her hand went absently to her waist, reaching for the comfort of her Glock. Nothing there. She hesitated for a fraction of a second. Better safe than sorry.

She went back into her room, made sure the door was latched, then retrieved her Glock 27 from its case in the interior of her suitcase. The key to the lock shook in her hands—damn, it was cold. She had only brought the small backup gun, certainly hadn't planned to get it from its case. She hadn't expected to need it, not at a conference in a swanky hotel.

She slapped a magazine in place, put two more in her jacket pocket, and stowed the weapon in a small belt-clipped holster. She felt sure she wouldn't be the only one armed out of this crew—cops and counterintelligence officers weren't that different.

More comfortable with the familiar weight on her hip, she left the room, followed the remaining stragglers to the stairwell.

"What's the matter?" she called out to the nearest man.

"Dunno," he replied. "Guess it's a fire. Wish they'd turn that bloody alarm off though, it's breaking my eardrums."

"No kidding. It's deafening."

Down the five flights, carefully picking their way, with cell phones giving the only decent light. There was emergency lighting on the walls, but the lights were dim, as if they weren't getting proper connections.

The stairwell exited into the lobby. A crowd of people had gathered in the dark. They weren't being evacuated, just left to mingle in the cavernous space.

Taylor didn't like this at all. She bumbled around in the dark a bit, saw Cherry, her face underlit by a flashlight, making her seem like a ghoul. She was pale and carrying a clipboard. Just as Taylor reached her, the alarm stopped, leaving her ears ringing.

Cherry gave her a wan smile. "Oh, good, Lieutenant Jackson. I can mark you off the list."

"What's going on? Is there a fire?"

"When the power went out, the generators to the rooms failed. A small fire started on the roof, and they're trying to contain it. There's a skeleton staff on the night shift, plus several people couldn't—or wouldn't—make the drive in, and the roads are blocked now, so the fire trucks can't get here. They're doing the best they can."

"Should we be evacuating people?"

"No, not yet. Thankfully, the lobby is on a separate generator, and the heat will stay on in here for a while. As soon as they give the word, we can send people back to their rooms. Might as well settle in until they give the all clear."

"You need to put me to work, I'm going bonkers. What can I do to help?"

Cherry flashed the light on her list. "We're still missing a few people. Would you be willing to take a flashlight and hike back upstairs, knock on doors? Be very careful, we wouldn't want you getting hurt."

"Absolutely. Who are we missing?"

"Let's see . . . Ellis Stamper—he's in 4880. And Thierry Florian, right next door in 4900. Hildy Rochelle, as well, the brunette woman who was charming everyone tonight. She's on the fifth floor, 5380."

The man nearest them said, "Cherry, I saw her earlier. She's down here somewhere."

"Oh, good. Thanks for letting me know, Ron." She turned back to Taylor. "Just the two gentlemen, then."

"Got it. On my way."

"Thank you, Taylor. I appreciate it."

Cherry handed Taylor an extra flashlight. She headed back to the stairwell.

Now that it was silent and empty, Taylor had to admit it was a little creepy. She climbed the stairs, enjoying the burn in her thighs that started on the third floor. It warmed her up. The faint scent of smoke was stronger up here, but no worse than when she'd exited her room.

The fourth floor was deserted. Taylor turned on the flashlight—it was amazing how dark the hallway had become. She heard nothing but the whistling wind.

Room 4880 was halfway down the hall. She knocked on the door.

"Excuse me, Mr. Stamper? You're needed downstairs."

Nothing.

She banged a few more times. He must have passed her in the night. She walked down to the room next door. "Mr. Florian, it's Taylor Jackson. The generators are out to the rooms, and there's a fire on the roof. They want everyone downstairs. Cherry sent me up to find you."

Silence again.

They must have already made their way down. A wasted trip.

She'd just started back toward the stairwell when she heard the noise.

She stopped dead in her tracks, listened for it. Yes, there it was again. It sounded like crying. She pulled open the stairwell door and let it slam closed, then stepped lightly back to the two men's rooms.

Stamper's room was still dead quiet, but she could swear there were hushed voices coming from Florian's.

She knocked again. "Mr. Florian? Are you in there?"

Nothing. The silence was pervasive, complete. False alarm?

She shook it off. Must have been the wind. Or, better yet, this old place was probably haunted, and she'd just been tricked by a ghost.

Not that she believed in ghosts.

Not really.

She went for the stairwell, made her way back down to the lobby. She found Cherry in the spot she'd left her.

"Nobody home. They must already be down here, and you just missed them."

Cherry's brow creased.

"They're not here, Taylor. I've talked to everyone, they are all in the room behind the lobby's entrance. There's a giant wood-burning fireplace in there, and plenty of logs. They've opened the bar, there's some water boiling for tea and hot chocolate. But everyone who went in passed by me, and I didn't see them."

"Well, that is weird. Let's go do a lap, see if they came late."

It took five minutes of flashing lights in strangers' eyes to see that there was no trace of either man.

Chapter 9

0230 Hours

Too close. Surely the woman won't come back, she will assume the bastard has already vacated his room.

I remember seeing her at the cocktail party, tall, blond, aloof. Looked frigid as hell. Pretty, if you liked the ice princess type. She gave off a whiff of danger, her eyes watching every move in the room. A cop, for sure. I've seen too many in my day not to be able to pick them from the crowd.

Florian is whimpering again. I kick him in the ribs. "Shut up, old man. We are not finished."

He is missing part of a finger, a play I wasn't planning to have to employ so early in our friendly chat. But he was not taking me seriously, so I had to make a point. It was the tip of his pinky, just a quick snip of the shears, but bloody, for all that.

I flash the light in his eyes, his pupils hurriedly shrink. He moans again.

"I will take the gag out if you promise to cooperate. To tell me what I want to know."

A nod.

"If you don't cooperate, there will be more fingers. Then toes, and hands, followed by your feet. *Tu comprends*? Do you understand?"

Another nod. I swear his skin pales—perhaps I've finally

made my point.

I remove the gag, dragging it down over his chin. He gulps for air. "They will come back. You can't get away with this."

"How disappointing. *Crétin. Maudite vache.* Do you not know who I am?"

He looks, uncomprehending. He does not know me in the darkness, in his confusion. Granted, I'm still in the brown wig from earlier, the dark contacts. A small adjustment to my nose.

I pull the wig from my head, and he gasps.

But it is not in recognition, it is in pain. He has passed out. I forget his age. He will not last the night at this rate. I must slow down.

His words penetrate. *They will come back.*

They will. I should move him. But where?

My finger taps against my thigh, and I hear his intake of breath. He is awake, and recognizes that small movement. Finally, he knows who he is dealing with.

"*Mon dieu.* Angelie. Angelie Delacroix. Is that you?"

"*Oui, Thierry. C'est moi. Je suis vivant, et tu êtes mort.*"

The knife slides into his ribs with ease, just above the kidneys. Not deep enough to be fatal. Not yet.

I whisper in his ear, the words harsh, metallic on my tongue. The question I've been waiting two and a half decades to ask.

"Why did you kill my father?"

Chapter 10

0400 Hours

Unintended consequences. The fire was contained, and everyone was given the okay to go back to their rooms. But without power, the electronic key cards wouldn't work. The generator that powered the rooms was damaged in the fire. Until the power was restored, they were stuck. The hotel staff was forced to gather everyone back in the lobby near the fireplace.

The generator to the first floor lobby ran out of fuel just after 4:00 a.m.

The depth of the snow was overwhelming. In just eight hours, there were at least four feet pushing up against the hotel's front door, and it was still coming down. Ice crackled along the windows, the moaning wind fighting to gain entry into the hotel. Cracks sounded in the distance, tree limbs collapsing under the sudden weight.

There was talk of evacuation, but Taylor knew that was a pipe dream—what were they going to do, bring a bus in? And where would they go? The entire eastern seaboard was caught in the grip of the storm. Nothing was moving. They were stuck here.

Cherry was waiting for a maintenance man to arrive with an override master key that would allow them access to rooms 4880 and 4900. She paced the lobby, staring out into the snow. Taylor figured she knew deep down there was no help coming.

Everyone knew something was wrong, that Thierry Florian and Ellis Stamper were missing. Whether they were in their rooms, or had left the premises and weren't able to return, no one knew. The idea of the two men caught out in that blizzard was unthinkable.

Stamper, it turned out, was also a member of the Macallan Group. He was Thierry's assistant, though that term was a misnomer. *Right-hand* would be more appropriate. *Bodyguard* might even come into play.

Their relationship had even been speculated about once or twice, though Florian put those vulgar rumors to rest quite openly, taking a beautiful young lover who'd ended up as his wife three years earlier. Stamper had married a year later as well.

It was their habit to get two-bedroom suites at hotels, ostensibly so Stamper could watch out over his boss. But for this event, the suites were booked, and they'd been forced into adjoining rooms instead. The front desk clerk remembered their conversation clearly, and the manager had sent a fruit basket to Mr. Florian to apologize for the mix-up.

There was no way to call either wife, to ask if she'd heard from her husband. No power, no cell service, no landlines. They were an island, in the dark and cold.

Taylor was chomping at the bit to get into the rooms. She wasn't in her jurisdiction, or she'd be ordering people around. Instead, the hotel staff was waiting for a representative from the Sheriff's office to show up before they opened the doors.

Precious moments ticking away. Modern technology was fantastic until the world was plunged into the dark, and then the Middle Ages again reigned supreme.

Taylor watched the minutes pass on her TAG Heuer watch, catching Cherry's eye every once in a while.

It took people who'd become accustomed to death to sense that this situation was very, very bad.

Chapter 11

0500 Hours

"Angelie. You must know, I did everything in my power to stop the murder. Your father, he would not listen. We begged him to stay put in Paris, that we had him covered, but he loaded up your mother and sister and you into the caravan and drove south. He thought he could protect you better than I. He was wrong."

"He was not wrong. He died protecting us. It was your job to keep him safe, to keep us all safe. He stole secrets for you, and you let him be gunned down. They killed my sister first, did you know that? Beatrice was six. Six, Florian—dead in my mother's lap. Her blood dripping into my hair."

"Is that what you're doing, Angelie? Systematically murdering all of the people involved in your father's case? Yes, I heard tonight about poor Gregoire Campion. I didn't realize you were capable of such an atrocity. You cut him into pieces and stowed his body in a duffel in his bathtub. The man was your friend, Angelie. How could you do that to him?"

I laugh. "A friend? Campion was never my friend. He used me, for years. Like all of you. His death is not on my conscience, Thierry. I did simply what I must to gain the truth, at last."

"*Alors*, Angelie, this is a pointless exercise. Murdering the minders will not bring your father back. It will not bring your family back. We did everything we could to protect them. In the end, the cause was simple. Your father trusted the wrong people."

Fury crowds into my chest. This is the lie Campion spewed when he was at the end. I slap Florian's face, hard.

"Lies. Don't even try to justify yourself. Oncle Pierre has shared the file with me, Thierry. I know exactly what happened. I know how you sold my father out to the Iraqis. He was the only one who had the capability to help them build their bloody bombs, and you told them where he would be that day."

His voice is soft in the darkness. "No, Angelie. That is wrong. We would never give your father to them. Never."

Florian goes silent. Something is not right here, I can feel it. I take a lap around the dark room, trying and failing to gather my temper. The cover-up is secure; all involved have the same story. How to get the truth? What will I have to do to this master of spies to find the answers I seek?

"Angelie. You've served your country admirably for fifteen years. You're one of the best assets we've ever had. Your future is bright. Why are you doing this? Why now, after all these years?"

I pull the crumbled paper from my purse. So many lives, so many sacrifices, all to procure this single sheet of paper.

I put it in front of his face, play a flashlight over the words.

He reads, then chews on his lip before he calmly sits back on the floor.

"Don't do this," he says, and there is no pleading in his voice, not like the others, who begged for their lives. Florian won't beg. He will find a way to go down swinging. He taught me that, at least.

I can't keep the tears from my voice. "I know, Thierry. I know it all."

Chapter 12

0600 Hours

The skies outside were dark gray. No power yet, but it wasn't the dead-of-night blackness from earlier. The mood in the room lightened, especially when the staff began handing out apples and bananas and granola bars, and stoked up the fire. If they just had some marshmallows, this would be more like a damn camping trip.

Taylor looked at her watch for the millionth time. "It's nearly six, Cherry. There's no more time to waste. It's been too long."

Cherry had dark circles below her eyes. She was clearly exhausted. But she came to life at Taylor's words, almost in relief. "I agree. I'm worried sick. Let's get the manager on duty, find out what the hell is happening."

At her wave, the hotel's manager on duty, a burly man named Fred, approached.

"Ma'am? Bad news. Our mechanic isn't going to make it. The Sheriff's office is responding to a huge wreck—buncha cars on the highway crashed, they can't spare anyone for at least an hour. We're stuck, I'm afraid."

"Fred, I'm sorry, but we need in those rooms. The Freedom Conference will pay for the damages we're about to incur."

"What?"

Taylor chimed in. “Can you let us into your maintenance room? We’re going to need some tools. A wrench and a screwdriver, for starters. A crowbar, if you have it.”

Fred’s brown creased. “Um, ma’am, just what are you planning to do?”

Taylor smiled. “Easy. Bust the locks off the doors.”

“I can’t let you do that. Those locks cost—”

“It doesn’t matter. There could be two lives at stake in there, and we’re not going to wait any longer.”

“I gotta talk to the main hotel property managers, they’re in Denver. They own the resort. I can’t let you—”

Taylor got in his face, her voice stern. “Fred, we aren’t going to wait. We will take responsibility. I’m a cop. You place the blame squarely on my head, and I’ll cover your back. The tools, now.”

People always backed down when she used that tone. Fred grabbed a flashlight, and, without a word, headed toward the back stairs.

“I’ve got this, Cherry. I’ll be back for you in a minute.”

It took five minutes to gather the tools she thought she’d need. Fred wasn’t talking, just shined the big industrial flashlight where Taylor asked. She’d scared him enough that he was keeping his mouth shut; she assumed he probably had a record he hadn’t disclosed, something minor, and didn’t want his bosses getting wind of his issues. She met guys like him in her investigations all the time. DUIs, late on their child support, warrants for traffic violations, gambling debts. Stupid stuff that should just be handled. Instead, they furtively tried to hide their misdeeds.

“Let’s go up. I might need your muscle,” she said, and Fred sullenly shined the light on the stairs for her. When they reached the first floor lobby, he stopped cold.

“You know what? You’re on your own from here. I ain’t going up there. I’m not going to be held responsible for this.”

Of course not.

“A noble speech, Fred. Thanks for doing the right thing.”

She left him gaping after her and found Cherry warming her hands near the fireplace. "I've got everything. Are you ready?"

"Yes," she said simply, and fell in line behind Taylor. The whispers started as they left the room.

As they climbed the stairs, the wind shrieked harder around the building, and its violent passage heightened the echoes of their footfalls in the darkened stairwell. It was even creepier than last night—Taylor sensed the storm was peaking. Hopefully, this would be the worst of it.

The fourth floor was eerily quiet. Once the stairwell door was shut, the wind's fury was muffled a bit.

The two women walked quickly down the hall. They stopped at Stamper's room first.

Taylor didn't move for a moment, just breathed deeply. All the hair stood up on the back of her neck. Something was different. Something was wrong.

"Do you smell that?"

Cherry nodded. She'd been around enough destruction, enough death, to recognize the scent.

"Blood," she whispered.

Taylor nodded. This wasn't going to end well, she could just feel it.

She took the crowbar to the door, not caring about the damage she was inflicting. With a great wrenching groan, the lock pulled free of the door. The metal warped, and Taylor used the screwdriver to wedge the tongue out of the bolt. It still didn't free, so she gave it a strong kick, and the door latch popped free.

She drew her weapon, took a flashlight from Cherry, and cross-armed the light under her shooting hand, the outside corners of each wrist meeting in a kiss.

The room was dark, the curtains pulled closed. Taylor swung the light around the room until she saw the body. The coppery tang of blood, a scent Taylor was much too familiar with, grew stronger the nearer she got to the bed.

Their worst fears, confirmed.

Cherry gasped aloud when she saw the neat hole in Ellis Stamper's forehead. The greatest damage was to the back of his skull, which had a massive hole in it where the bullet exited.

"Jesus. He's been executed."

Taylor said nothing, just moved the flashlight around the room, taking in the scene. He was naked on the bed, the sheets twisted. Underlying the blood was the scent of musk. Taylor approached the body, shined her flashlight up and down the length of him. There was a spent condom in the trashcan next to the bed.

"He had company."

Cherry joined her. "Conference sex. Happens all the time. We should make sure this doesn't get back to his wife." She reached for the condom; Taylor stopped her.

"What are you doing? We don't touch anything. If you persist I'll escort you from the room. Do you understand?"

Cherry gave Taylor a sad little smile. "I was COS for twenty years. My first responsibility is to my people."

"Not to the law, not to justice? You're willing to cover this up? Whoever he screwed most likely killed him."

"This will ruin him. His family, his honor—"

"Cherry, the man's dead. I daresay he's already ruined. Let's worry about soothing hurt feelings if the time comes. There's DNA on that condom, a piece of the puzzle we can't pretend doesn't exist. Get it?"

"Cops. Always afraid to do the right thing." There was a note of exasperated humor in Cherry's voice, which was a good thing, but Taylor gave her a baleful eye anyway, and she moved away from the bed.

The flashlight pummeled the darkness once more, and Taylor spied the connecting door to the next room. She thought about the room set up, realized it went to 4900.

"Cherry, look. This goes into Florian's room. Easier to get through this than tearing the electronic lock off the other door."

"I agree. But Taylor, be careful."

"*Careful* is my middle name."

Taylor eased the door open with her shoulder; it wasn't locked, or fully closed. Unlocked she could understand; if Stamper was Florian's bodyguard, he would need access to the room. And if the rumors were true, and they *were* lovers? That logic was sound; the used condom spoke volumes. Could Florian have shot his lover in a fit of rage, then left the hotel?

On the surface, that felt plausible, though not exactly right. Taylor hadn't gotten the violent vibe from Florian; he seemed more like an earnest schoolteacher than a bully.

She shone the flashlight closer on the lock. There were scratches, like an impatient thief had jimmied it open. So much for that theory.

She took a deep breath and called his name quietly.

"Mr. Florian?"

Silence.

"Shine the light around, Taylor."

She did, and wasn't surprised to find the room empty.

Chapter 13

0615 Hours

Florian has fainted, again. Before he succumbed to the pain, he was talking, but not saying the things I needed to hear. There are answers here, I know it. My father was not a traitor. My family did not have to die.

Many years of espionage has taught me well; eventually, everyone breaks. Watching Florian bleed and cry and lie isn't enough. I will speed up the process.

I go to the bathroom, gather a handful of water from the sink. The stream sputters and runs out as I watch. The room is cold; my hands are clumsy in the dark. Without the power, this is more difficult than I planned. The leads tied to Florian's chest and testicles will not work without electricity, and the fear of pain will not suffice. There has to be actual stimulus to coerce statements. Which means I'm back to the knife.

I splash the meager handful of water in his face, but it is enough. He sputters and his eyes open. I stand with my arms crossed, waiting for him to again register who I am, and why we are here.

"Angelie," he moans.

I drop to my knees, cajoling now, friendly.

"Talk to me, Thierry. Tell me what I need to know."

I wrap his wounds, binding them against the bleeding. It will feel better that way. He head lolls against me. I smell his fear. The infamous Thierry Florian, helpless and scared.

"That is all I have, Angelie. I know nothing else."

Kneeling back on my heels, I watch him. The letter tells me he is still lying.

"Thierry, they'll come for you soon. You must tell me the rest. Tell me, and this pain will stop." I tug on a lead attached between his legs, and he gulps a breath. His head bobs side to side, a metronome of hurt.

He whispers, "I would tell you you're wrong, but you will not believe me. "

"No, I won't believe anything less than the truth. You've been lying to me this entire time. For fifteen years, you've looked me in the face, knowing you killed my father. How could you? I thought you were my friend. I thought you were my father's friend."

He sighs, a great, dragging breath. "Dear Angelie, I am not lying. Your father panicked. We had a safe house prepared, guards to keep him safe, but someone got to him. Convinced him he was being double-crossed. Angelie, I do not know who this person was."

"Whoever it was, he told the truth. You double-crossed my father. You left him out in the cold to die." I toy with the knife at the edge of his groin. A lesser man would beg, plead, promise me anything, just to get the sharp edge away from their skin. Florian merely shakes his head.

"No, no, Angelie. I would never do that to him. He was my friend, yes, but I will be honest. He was too valuable. He was the greatest asset I'd ever trained. But the others, they had no compunction about lying to him to get what they wanted. And he chose to believe their faint words of promise, rather than follow my protocols. I wanted you all in the safe house in Annecy, he chose to buy the caravan and stay in the campgrounds. There was no way to protect him, he was too exposed. He exposed you all, and panicked when they came for him."

"More lies. This letter is dated three days before his death. He says he knew you were working for the Soviets. That you were a double agent. That's why he didn't trust you." I catch my tone, a petulant child. I add a sneer. "You dishonored your vows, Thierry, and their blood is on your hands."

Chapter 14

0630 Hours

Taylor's theory about Florian being the shooter changed when she saw the blood by the window.

"Cherry, over here."

"Oh, no. This goes from bad to worse."

"It does, but don't lose hope just yet. There's not enough blood to assume the worst, not by a long shot. This is just a thimbleful, really." Taylor stared at the blood drops. They were drying around the edges, though the centers were still wet. Not fresh, but not old, either.

"The storm kicked into high gear at midnight. A time of death on Mr. Stamper would go a long way toward telling us whether Florian is still on site or was taken from the hotel."

Cherry shook her head. "You're not making me feel better. I have one man down, and one missing. Where the hell could he be?"

Taylor tucked her weapon back into its holster.

"I don't know. Anywhere—this campus is huge. But if he's still here, you're missing the bigger picture."

"The bigger picture?"

"It's entirely possible we're locked in this hotel with a cold-blooded murderer."

Cherry sat down hard on Florian's bed. "Oh, Lieutenant,

trust me, I am well aware of this."

There was something in her tone, in the self-defeated flop on the bed.

Taylor squatted on the floor in front of the woman. "You sound like a woman who needs to get a load off her chest."

"I've screwed up. I didn't protect him. It's my fault."

"What do you mean, you've screwed up? Cherry, talk to me. What's really going on here?"

"You know who Thierry Florian is, I suspect?"

"He's worked with my fiancé, but I don't know him. I just met him tonight. He told me he's the head of the Macallan Group, and former clandestine services. The French, right, DGSE?"

"Always shy with his accomplishments, Thierry. That's what makes him such an excellent spy. His father was a leader in the French *Résistance* during World War II. When the French needed information about the Germans, François Florian would put himself in the worst possible situations, get arrested, then find ways to keep himself alive while he gathered information. When he had what he needed, he would escape and bring the information back to the resistance."

"An impressive man."

"Yes. Thierry was his youngest child, born well after the end of the war, but the tales his family told were intoxicating. While the rest of his siblings went into safe positions as doctors and lawyers, Thierry followed in his father's footsteps and joined what was then known as the DGSE—the Directorate-General for External Security."

"The French version of our CIA."

"Correct. He had an illustrious career. When he retired, he was the equivalent of our Director of Counterintelligence. But it was an especially covert side job that put him on his current path. Before he left he worked with the Alliance Base—do you know what that is?"

"An international cooperative of intelligence agencies,

right? Working against Al Qaeda and other terrorist organizations?"

"Yes." She smiled, a little sadly. "Thierry has always ruffled feathers in the intelligence community with his theories. He feels cooperative intelligence is vital to deter more terrorist attacks on the Western world. But putting a bunch of spies together—well, friction was inevitable. He saw the ways the organization worked, and the ways it didn't. He was determined to perfect the mix. Hence, The Macallan Group."

"Why are you telling me this, Cherry? The man's CV isn't necessary for me to want to help."

"Bear with me a few moments more, Taylor. Thierry has made many enemies, and he is a target. It is entirely possible we have been infiltrated by someone he pissed off back in the day, and they're taking their chance at retribution."

"You handpicked the conference members, though, didn't you? Surely you wouldn't be so careless as to let a known combatant in."

She gave a little moan. "Spies, Taylor, we're all spies. Everyone working at cross-purposes. It's why I don't work with Thierry at Macallan. I have a clearer head than he when it comes to the simple fact that for centuries, we've been working against each other. It's all well and good to hope for cooperation, but ultimately, someone will want to get payback for some perceived grievance, and it all collapses."

"So who here had a vendetta against Thierry?"

"I don't know."

"Cherry, think. If you truly believe the killer is a part of the conference, think!"

Cherry went quiet, then, in a small voice, said, "There's one other person unaccounted for. Not from the conference, from our lives. I've known her for years. She is a friend, of sorts. Used to be a protégé of Thierry's before she went out on her own. We've worked in some pretty hairy places together. She went off grid a year ago, just when Thierry formed The Macallan Group. He wanted to recruit her, came looking, but I hadn't heard from her in several months. We put out some feelers, to see if anyone knew where she was. She was for hire, you see, a black market baby, very hush-hush."

Taylor knew what *for hire* meant. "She's an assassin."

Cherry leapt from the bed at the word, shaking her head. "I was silly to bring it up. There's no way she could be involved in this. She fights against evil. That's what drives her."

"I take it the feelers came up empty?"

"Yes. Nothing. She's gone gray."

"Gray?"

"Blending in. Hiding in plain sight. She's most likely setting up for a major job."

Taylor's voice rose. "A major job? Come on Cherry, talk to me. What kind of major job would this woman have to disappear for a year to prepare for?"

Cherry just shook her head. "I don't know. Before she left, she'd been . . . reckless. Taking on jobs that were out of character."

A sense of foreboding crept into Taylor's stomach. International assassins on the loose made her very uncomfortable—she'd come face to face with one herself a year earlier and hadn't enjoyed it a lick. A different tact was necessary; she could see Cherry was shutting down.

"Tell me this. Something about this set-up makes you think of this woman. What is it?"

Cherry pursed her lips. "Thierry alluded once, only once, that there was history between them. She still worked for DGSE then, was being groomed to move up the ladder. Something set her off and she went freelance, and I've never known what it was. But Thierry did. He must have. That's what he meant when he told me she'd become a black widow."

Ah. Interesting. "She'd get physically close to her prey,

then kill them."

"Exactly. And she's one of the best at what she does. She's a legend, Taylor."

A legendary assassin. A wicked snowstorm. No power. One dead, one missing. This was just getting better and better.

"I take it the scene in Stamper's room looks familiar?"

"Very."

Taylor took the flashlight, went to the door, unlocked the bolt. Opened it into the dark hallway, then shined the light back into the room. There was no more time to lose.

"I need a name, Cherry."

The harsh light caught Cherry's face. She looked frightened and old, defeated, a pale specter in the darkness. She sat back down on the bed as if exhausted.

"She goes by many names, Taylor. But I believe her given name is Angelie Delacroix."

"That's a start. Let's go. We need to—"

Cherry shook her head, clearly the truth of the matter was finally sinking in. "No, Lieutenant, we have a bigger problem."

"Worse than one dead and one missing? Seriously?"

"Angelie's uncle is active MI-6. And he's downstairs."

Chapter 15

0640 Hours

I sit down on the floor near Florian. "Oncle Pierre told me the whole story last year. You were on the scene. You were the one who saved me, who took me to the hospital. But first you smashed me on the head so I wouldn't recognize you. Why did you kill my father, Thierry? My family? Why would you kill them and save me? *Pourquoi? Pourquoi?*"

I am shouting, losing control. I resist the urge to hit him again.

"Angelie. Angelie, it wasn't me. You have the story wrong."

I am beginning to believe Thierry Florian may be telling the truth. He is a proud man, one I've watched interrogate a hundred men. He is brave. And as he sits here bleeding, exposed, I must believe I know him well enough to recognize when he is telling the truth.

"Then what is the story, Thierry?"

"Don't make me tell you. Please."

This last word is spoken as softly as a lover's kiss. Finally, after hours of pain and fury, the great man is begging.

I tuck the muzzle of my Sig Sauer against his chin, and I raise his head so he is forced to meet my eyes.

"Tell me, and I will end your suffering."

He leans into the gun, his voice the harshest I've ever

heard. "Kill me, and you will never get justice."

I stand and whirl away. Florian breathes out a sigh.

"You will not stop, will you? Ah, Angelie. I trained you well."

I run back to him, wrench his head back. Spit the words. "The truth, now. I am sick of playing this game."

"Pierre," he says, speaking out loud a terrible reality I've never fathomed. "It was Pierre. Your uncle killed your father."

Nausea overwhelms me. I drop my hand. "You're lying."

Florian shakes his head. He is disheveled, bloody, has absolutely nothing left to lose.

"I have never lied to you, Angelie. I have protected you, all along. I did not want you to suffer the pain of this knowledge. Indeed, I sheltered you from it since you were a child. Yes, it was I who rescued you. I got wind of your uncle's plan the day before the attack, though at the time I did not know he was behind it. I was in Germany. I drove all night to reach you, to take you all to safety.

"Your father ignored our attempts to get him into the safe house in Annecy. He was fleeing back to Paris on Pierre's orders. He believed Pierre was trying to help. He listened to him, and drove directly into the trap."

I stagger against the wall, tripping on something in the darkness. A pain I have not felt in twenty-five years rises in me, tears through my body, my brain, leaving me breathless.

"This cannot be the truth."

"It is the truth. I arrived on the scene moments after the shooting. Gregoire Campion was riding his bicycle down from the safe house, he met me on the westbound street. We were too late to save them, Angelie, too late by five minutes. But you were still alive, clinging to your mother's skirts, covered in your parents' blood. I couldn't leave you there, and I could not let you see our faces. I did the only thing I could, which was rescue you and get you to a hospital. And I spent the next twenty years trying to determine what happened that day."

I try to digest this information.

"Why did you not tell me the moment you determined Pierre was behind the execution?"

"Ah. Angelie. And cause you that much more pain? Your uncle raised you, taught you well. He knew where your heart lay, knew you would try to avenge your parents some day. He is the reason you were hired into the DGSE. Gregoire Campion was worried about you from the first because he suspected Pierre's involvement, kept an eye on you, eased your path in the service. And you killed him. The man who watched over you, dead by your hand. Angelie, you disgrace yourself."

Campion, on the side of the angels?

I harden myself against Florian's words. "Pierre told me Campion was the one who let my parents' path slip, that he told the Iraqis where my father was going to be that day."

"That was Pierre, *mon cherie*. Pierre was receiving money, so much money, that he was willing to sacrifice his brother and his family. He has lied to you, Angelie, about many things. I am not a double agent. And I did not kill your father."

There is great finality to his words. I know he is telling the truth.

I slide down the wall, the pistol dangling between my legs.

Mon dieu. What have I done?

Chapter 16

0645 Hours

Taylor hustled down the four flights of stairs, Cherry on her heels. The minute they reached the bottom floor, Taylor asked, "What does he look like?"

"Mid-sixties, silver hair, six feet or so. He was wearing a blue suit last night, no tie, but I don't remember what he was wearing this morning. It was dark, and I was too concerned for Thierry and Ellis."

They burst into the lobby, raced to the room where everyone was staged. The room was still shrouded in darkness, and there was no more time to waste.

"Stay here. I'll find him."

"But you don't know what he looks like."

Taylor flashed the light on the ceiling a few times, creating a strobe effect that caught people's attention.

"Pierre Matthews. Are you in here?" she called.

Murmurs from the crowd, then one man stood, Taylor could see the outline of his bulk against the window.

"I'm here. Whatever is the matter?"

Taylor crossed the room, weaving between people, and took him by the arm. "Come with me, please, sir. There's a problem. We need your help."

The lobby was filled with natural light, the darkness finally easing in the early morning sun. The snow, she noticed, had stopped. Taylor turned off the flashlight, tucked it into her back pocket.

"What is this about?" Matthews asked.

"Sir, I'm Lieutenant Taylor Jackson, and you know Cherry Gregg. We have reason to believe you may be in danger. Would you please come with us?"

Matthews was nonplussed, but nodded. Taylor took the lead, Cherry flanked. They got him across into the bar, and Taylor got him into a corner where she felt he would be safest.

"You two have been scurrying in and out all night. What's happened? Where are Thierry and Ellis?"

Cherry spoke plainly. "Ellis is dead, and Thierry is missing."

"Bloody hell. Are you sure?"

"Do you know a woman named Angelie Delacroix?" Taylor asked.

Matthews sucked in a breath, and Taylor raised an eyebrow. "I'll take that as a yes."

She saw him debating with the answer. Finally, he replied, "She's my niece. Why are you asking about her? Is she all right?"

Cherry grabbed the man's forearm. "Pierre, she killed Ellis. She's taken Thierry."

Pierre froze. "Angelie is here? Are you sure?"

"Yes. She knows."

Taylor gave Cherry a sharp look. "She knows what?"

Cherry and Pierre were locked in a staring contest, no words needed. Taylor recognized there was a bigger issue, something major they were keeping from her.

"Tell me right now what's happening, or I'm out. I'll go warm my hands by the fire and let Fred shoot me dirty looks."

Cherry nodded to Pierre. "You tell her."

"Ah, bugger me." He rubbed his hands over his face, the whiskers on his chin rasping loudly against his palm. "Angelie started acting up about two years ago. She didn't like the politics within the DGSE anymore, didn't want to play by the rules. We were all working together at the time, on the Allied project. The greater good. CIA, MI-6, DGSE, Freedom Forum, Futures Working Group—hell, even Pakistan's ISI was along for the ride. In the middle of the fuck-up in Benghazi, she got a bug up her bum about some old case, took off for parts unknown. All we've heard from her since has been at the end of a gun—she's left a trail of bodies all over Europe, the last one found just two days ago in London."

"Gone rogue?" Taylor couldn't help the skepticism that slipped into her tone.

"That's right. You must understand, Lieutenant, Angelie is marked by tragedy. Her parents were killed in an ambush outside Annecy, France, twenty-five years ago. She was the only survivor, and she spent her whole life searching for the killers."

Taylor heard the past tense. "*Spent* her whole life? She's found her parents' murderers?"

He cut his eyes at Cherry, who nodded imperceptibly. "She found him at last. Gregoire Campion, her latest victim, the body from two days ago. She found a letter with the details. He sold out her parents, my own brother, and for what? Money? Security? Who can know the true heart of a man like that, Lieutenant? I am sure his death assuaged many of Angelie's troubles."

Taylor processed that for a moment. "If she found the man who did it, then why would she come here and kill Ellis Stamper? Why kidnap Thierry Florian?"

"Stamper was most likely collateral damage. Florian worked with Campion back then. He was the DGSE equivalent of a station chief in Geneva, Switzerland, just north of Annecy. She must think he was a part of the plot."

"Was he?" Taylor asked, trying to reconcile this information against her brief meeting with Florian and Cherry's praise-filled backgrounder. He didn't seem capable of that level of treachery. Taylor prided herself on being able to read people; she hadn't caught a whiff of evil from Florian.

"I don't know. He denied it, said he was there trying to protect them, but I never got the whole story. My brother's death was a terrible time for us all. I took Angelie in, raised her as my own daughter. She had a massive memory block on what happened that day—after the head injury, it was all gone. She took a hard blow, probably pistol-whipped. It was a miracle that she survived. Florian had his eye on her from the very beginning. You know what they say: keep your friends close, but keep your enemies closer."

Taylor didn't like Pierre Matthews. He was slick; the answers were too pat, too prepared, and something in her gut told her he was lying. Granted, a situation like this, about family, so personal, there was no reason to tell her the whole truth. Yes, he was lying. She'd bet her life on it. About what, she didn't know, and that made him very dangerous to her in this situation. And she realized Cherry knew more than she was letting on, too.

"Are you armed, Pierre?"

"My weapon is in my room. Why?"

Thank God for small favors.

"Well, your friend, or your enemy, is missing, and Cherry believes it's likely your niece is prowling around this hotel with her own loaded weapon. We need to figure out where Thierry Florian is, and take your niece into custody while we assess what happened last night."

Cherry came back to life, finally. "Without lights for those dark hallways, or the ability to open multiple doors without tearing this place apart, how do we search?"

Taylor shrugged. "We need to find a way to get the lights turned on."

Chapter 17

0650 Hours

I unbind Florian's ties, my fingers working quickly. It would have been so easy to simply kick his chair, let him fall into the pool. He would have been gone, his storied life a sudden footnote, the weight of the chair keeping him under.

There will be no more deaths, save one.

Florian stands cautiously, rubbing his wrists.

"Clothes?"

I gesture to the right, by the hot tub, where his clothes are folded in a neat pile. He says nothing, simply turns his back on me and dresses. I walk slowly, carefully, around the edges of the pool. It would be so easy to fling myself into the dark water. It is salt water; I can smell the brine. Like floating in an ocean, sinking deep beneath the waves. My parents used to take us to the sea, to Le Lavendou, and we'd stay at the Beau Rivage and prune ourselves in the azure water from sunup to sundown.

I did not know these holidays were paid for by secrets. Blueprints and plans for rapidly-developed forms of kinetic energy, stolen by my father from his employer, and sold to the Iraqis. Or the Russians. Syrians and Pakistanis. Whoever was paying at that particular moment.

My father was a mole. An asset. Turned for the DGSE's

use, a puppet on a string, only useful while he could help in the race to nuclear proliferation supremacy.

And me? I became the very person my father hated. The nameless, faceless people he put his trust in, the mechanics of his dead drops and microfiche holders and tradecraft.

I could not help it. *Mon oncle,* he showed me how valuable this work was. How I could change the world, one turned asset at a time.

If my father lived, would that have changed? Would I have been so heavily recruited? So well-trained? Honed into a weapon of immeasurable worth?

I think not.

Florian is watching me. “Angelie. You must leave.”

My toe yanks back from the water. I stare into Florian’s eyes, unable to see clearly for the lack of light.

“Go. I will handle this situation. Get away from this place.”

“Why would you have me save myself, Thierry Florian? Why should I not turn myself in? Suffer the consequences of my actions? I have killed this night. Taken your friend from you. You should want my head.”

He smiles, the tiniest lift of the corners of his mouth. And I know what he will say next.

“What a curious turn of phrase. *Oui, cherie,* I very much want your head. And I shall have it. You work for me now, Angelie. Again. Again and forever. Now, go.”

I am defeated. For a moment I think to kill him anyway. Then I can be free. But I listen.

I stash the gun in my waistband, gather my tools, and without a word, head for the door. There is a storm. I know this; I see the piles of snow against the door. How I will get away isn’t clear. I had no plans for escape. This was intended to be my last hurrah. A suicide mission. But now that I know the truth? As they say, the show must go on.

The hallways are still dark and quiet. The blueprint of the hotel plays through my head. I need to turn left at the gym, it will lead me to the basement, which has an exit onto a back expanse of land. There is a shelter one hundred yards from the hotel, a place I can regroup until I can reach my exit.

A voice from the other side of the pool. "Hey. Hey, stop!"

My weapon is pointed at the voice before I can form a coherent thought.

Chapter 18

0700 Hours

A fuel truck, riding slowly behind a snowplow, arrived at seven in the morning to everyone's cheers. The fuel was pumped into the basement generators, the lights flickered to life, and a semblance of normality restored. People scattered back to their rooms to get some sleep and check in with loved ones.

Taylor was glad of it; now they could do a proper search, and run a crime scene unit through Stamper and Florian's rooms.

Cherry and Pierre had been huddled together in a corner of the bar for the past fifteen minutes, backs to the wall, eyes darting to the entrance every few moments, and Taylor wondered what sort of story they were concocting. Self-preservation, preparation, a cover-up, she didn't know, only that they were both acting like Angelie Delacroix was going to burst through the wall yelling *yippie ki-yay* and shoot up the place.

Taylor left them alone, paced the bar. Florian's disappearance was gnawing at her. She wanted to strike off and look for him, but knew how foolish that was, especially if the über-assassin was still on site. They needed manpower, backup, K9 units, the works. Sure enough, fifteen minutes later, the Calvert County Sheriff, a decent-looking man named Evans, arrived, summoned by the report of a murder.

Taylor and Cherry explained the situation. To his credit, he took down their stories with a raised eyebrow and only a few head shakes. He went upstairs, came down with a grim expression, asked Taylor several probing questions, then said, "Lieutenant, glad you were here. Situation might have gotten further out of control. There are more people coming, State Police, FBI, K9. Storm's holding everyone up. We're going to need you to give your official statement, so get comfy."

"Can't I help? I don't want to sit around doing nothing."

"It's going to take more than two of us to search this place." He smiled, kindly enough. "You've done your part. Why don't you head to your room and get some rest? I'd lock my door, though my guess is Florian and this Delacroix woman are long gone. Timing wise, the streets were still passable until after midnight. The hotel lobby's videotape wasn't recording, so that's useless. Just need to bring in the troops and get this place searched and processed. You know how it goes."

Taylor did, and knew her role in the situation was finished. With the jurisdictional cops on scene, she was relegated back to conference attendee and witness. Which was weird.

But Evans had a point. A little sleep wouldn't go amiss.

She interrupted another confab between Pierre and Cherry.

"Cherry, I'm going to go up to my room. Call me if they find Florian, okay?"

Chapter 19

0730 Hours

Taylor had to detour to her room—though the power was back on, the elevators were still off-limits. She pulled a site map off the concierge desk and glanced at it. The back staircase would be closer to her room. She took the hallway toward the gym, the scent leading her toward the pool and the hot tub. Ah, a hot bath in that giant tub upstairs would be lovely, though she doubted the water heaters were going to get suitable power from the generators to pump water hot enough for her taste.

She pushed through the pool doors and immediately knew something was wrong. Instinct, coupled with the chair at the edge of the pool, ropes coiled neatly by its legs. She drew her weapon and went into a defensive stance. The glass windows in the place were wavy, giving weak light that shimmered against the pool water. She went slowly, searching, until she saw the open door to the lifeguard office. And inside was Thierry Florian, eyes closed, leaning back on a longue chair. Blood soaked his shirt, and he was pale as a ghost. Asleep, or dead?

She rushed to him, put her fingers against his carotid. A steady beat, and her breath whooshed out. He started, eyes opening. "Angelie, I told you—"

He cut himself off when he saw Taylor.

"Where is she?"

"I don't know what you're talking about."

"Mr. Florian, please. Ellis Stamper is dead. You've obviously been tortured. I know all about Angelie Delacroix. Cherry and Pierre Matthews filled me in. Where is she?"

He licked his lips, which were cracked and bloody. "Gone," he whispered.

She helped him sit up.

"Why aren't you dead? It looks like she gave you quite a working over."

He smiled, though the action obviously caused him pain. "You are blunt, aren't you, Lieutenant? Angelie didn't want me dead. She just wanted information."

"Somehow, I don't believe that is the whole story. The Sheriff is here, and there's about to be a whole wad of law enforcement on his tail. Is she still here, Thierry? Tell me the truth."

"She left ten minutes ago. You won't catch her."

Taylor met his eyes. "Watch me."

Chapter 20

0735 Hours

Taylor called Cherry, told her to share what was happening with the Sheriff, and to send backup immediately. She shoved her cell phone in her pocket and press checked her Glock. It was habit, a cop's unconscious movement.

Florian tried to stop her. "You're wasting your time."

He tried to rise, but the blood loss had taken its toll.

"You stay here and guard the pool. When the Sheriff's people come, show them the way."

"On your head be it," Florian said. "Don't say I didn't warn you."

Taylor gave him a smile and started off.

One thing Taylor had gathered about Angelie Delacroix, there would be signs of her passage. Morbid signs. Since Taylor hadn't seen any on her way in, she exited opposite the door she'd originally come through, toward the north end of the pool, right out into the hallway that led to the back entrance of the hotel. The light was startling here, she had to blink to adjust.

She took in the whiteness outside, knew there was no way anyone could get out of there without leaving a mess.

It didn't take long to find the trail. Footprints led toward a small outbuilding about fifty yards away. Backup was moments behind, so Taylor stepped out into the freezing cold.

Her hands went numb almost immediately, but she kept the weapon up and ready. The going was slow, the snow drifting to her waist in places. The chill wind was rising again, Taylor recognized the feeling. This was a temporary reprieve; there was more snow on the way.

Her feet were snug in her boots, but snow was sliding down the calf and into the leather. A fine shiver started, and with it, her common sense.

You're an idiot, Taylor. Go back inside and let the locals freeze their asses off.

She could hear them now, closing in. She started edging backwards. As she turned, there was a woman, standing in her path.

Taylor froze. The woman was small—Taylor had a good six inches on her—but her weapon was pointed right at Taylor's head.

"And who might you be?" the woman asked, her accent clearly French.

"Police. Put the gun down, Angelie. You can't rack up any more bodies today, you're already going away for a very long time."

The woman cocked her head to the side. The gun didn't waver.

"I think you are the one who needs to disarm yourself, Lieutenant Jackson. Yes, I know your name. It's next to that smiling photograph on the program in Thierry's room. A profiler, are you?"

"Homicide. You're under arrest. Put the damn gun down, now."

"I think not," Angelie said, then before Taylor could blink, she took off, through the snow, toward a stone wall that barely peeked out under its white blanket.

"Shit!"

Taylor took off after her, amazed at Angelie's prowess in the snow. Taylor was too tall, too ungainly, to make quick progress. There was only one thing to do.

Taylor stopped and fired, and the bullet found its target. Angelie spun to the side, and Taylor heard her cry out.

"Drop the weapon, Angelie, and I won't do that again."

Shouts rang out from the building to her left, the Sheriff's deputies were coming. Angelie heard them as well, didn't hesitate. She fired off several rounds, spraying them wildly behind her, forcing Taylor face down in the snow.

Taylor rolled to her right, flipped over and up onto her knees and aimed again.

Angelie's left arm was dragging by her side, but she kept running, a dead sprint through the heavy snow. She reached the stone wall before Taylor could get off a second round, and disappeared behind it.

It took Taylor a full minute to scramble to her feet and reach the spot.

"She's here," she called to the deputies, who were wading through the snow well behind her.

Carefully, slowly, weapon first, Taylor looked over the edge of the wall. Beyond it was a steep slope. It was terraced, a vineyard in the summertime, staggered levels that ran down the hill, demarcated by stone barriers. One section dropped off into the beach below. Taylor figured it must be a forty-foot drop.

Angelie Delacroix was crouched against the stone barrier above the beach, back to the ocean, watching Taylor. She was trapped, and bleeding. Their eyes met.

Taylor edged closer. *Take the shot, Taylor, take the shot. You can end this, right here.*

She took a breath to steady her hands, shaking in the cold. Her finger rested on the trigger. Just a fraction of movement, and the bullet would take Angelie Delacroix in the forehead.

And in that moment, Angelie raised her weapon toward Taylor in a sort of salute and smiled, crooked, knowing, then jumped off the ledge, toward the sea.

Taylor gritted her teeth and scrambled over the wall. *Damn it. Damn it all.* She'd had a clear shot. She shouldn't have hesitated. But she recognized something in the woman's eyes. Something dark, and unimaginable to those who hadn't been faced with taking a life. And Taylor had chosen that route, too many times.

The first bullet had hit Angelie in the shoulder. Taylor had shot to maim, not kill. She made a choice, right or wrong, and now her prey was gone.

She pointed the weapon at the barrier, just where the woman had disappeared. Listened, but heard nothing.

"Police!" she shouted. "Show me your hands."

Silence. The waves crashed below, a seagull cried. Silence amplified by the dizzying expanse of white before her, her voice echoed slightly. To her right, disturbed by the deputies making their way closer, a bird took wing, startled by the noise, sent her heart right to her throat.

Taylor ducked her head, took a deep breath in through her nose, and leading with her Glock, looked over the edge. She was prepared for what she found.

Nothing.

There was no sign of Angelie Delacroix.

All that was left of her was a spattering of blood drops on the snow, like a shower of rubies dashed onto white velvet.

When Taylor had hesitated, that split second when she decided she couldn't kill, not again, something like realization had dawned in Angelie's eyes. She had recognized that Taylor would not fire again.

That knowing smile would haunt Taylor's dreams.

A choice. Right or wrong, Taylor had let her get away.

She slumped against the stone. The deputies finally reached her, Sheriff Evans at their head.

"Where is she, where is she?"

"She jumped."

Evans looked slightly relieved, holstered his weapon.

"Then she's dead. That's a fifty-foot fall. We'll find her

body on the beach."

"I don't think so," she said, and he looked at her queerly.

"Of course we will. What the hell were you doing, out here chasing her down alone? I thought I told you to stand down."

Taylor turned to face him, the wind whipping her hair around her face.

"I was doing my job."

And the sun broke through the clouds.

Epilogue

January 15, 2014
London, England
0300 Hours

I stand over his bed. He sleeps with one arm tossed over his head. I recognize the position; my father, his brother, also slept in this way—careless, with abandon.

He is quiet. No snoring, just deep, rhythmic breaths.

I want him to see. I want him to know. I rub my shoulder, warding off the pain from the ghost of a bullet that lodged against my scapula, courtesy of the blonde ice queen. I'll never forget, and she knew that would be the case. But I will leave her alone. I have learned a hard truth in the past few months.

Not all scores are meant to be settled.

But some . . . some beg for closure.

I slide his covers down with the end of my weapon, and lean close, so I can whisper in his ear.

"Oncle Pierre. Time to wake up."

STORM SEASON—ONE STORM. THREE NOVELLAS.
BONUS MATERIAL
MEET THE AUTHORS
CHAPTER EXCERPTS

MEET J.T. ELLISON

New York Times bestselling author **J.T. Ellison** writes dark psychological thrillers starring Nashville Homicide Lt. Taylor Jackson and medical examiner Dr. Samantha Owens, and pens the Nicholas Drummond series with #1 *New York Times* bestselling author Catherine Coulter. Co-host of the premier literary television show, *A Word on Words*, Ellison lives in Nashville with her husband and twin kittens.

For more insight into her wicked imagination, join J.T.'s email list at jtellison.com/subscribe, or follow her online at Face-book.com/JTEllison14 or on Twitter @thrillerchick.

MEET ALEX KAVA

Alex Kava is the *New York Times* and International bestselling author of the critically acclaimed Maggie O'Dell series and a new series featuring former Marine, Ryder Creed and his K-9 dogs

Her stand-alone novel, *One False Move*, was chosen for the 2006 One Book One Nebraska and her political thriller, *Whitewash*, was one of *January Magazine's* best thrillers of the year. Her novel, *Stranded* was awarded both a Florida Book Award and the Nebraska Book Award.

Published in over thirty-three countries, Alex's novels have made the bestseller lists in the UK, Australia, Germany, Japan, Italy and Poland.

She is currently working on BEFORE EVIL, a prequel to A Perfect Evil, and LOST CREED, the next in-line of the Creed series.

MEET ERICA SPINDLER

Erica Spindler is the *New York Times* and International Chart bestselling author of thirty-two novels and three eNovellas. Spindler's skill for crafting engrossing plots and compelling characters has earned both critical praise and legions of fans. Published across the globe, she's been called "The Master of Addictive Suspense" and "The Queen of the Romantic Thriller."

Her most recent novels are THE FINAL SEVEN and TRIPLE SIX, books one and two in her *The Lightkeepers* series.

Spindler splits her writing time between her New Orleans area home and a lakeside writing retreat. She's married to her college sweetheart, has two sons and the constant companionship of Roxie, *the wonder retriever*.

She is busy writing her next thriller, THE OTHER GIRL and FALLEN FIVE, book three in *The Lightkeepers*.

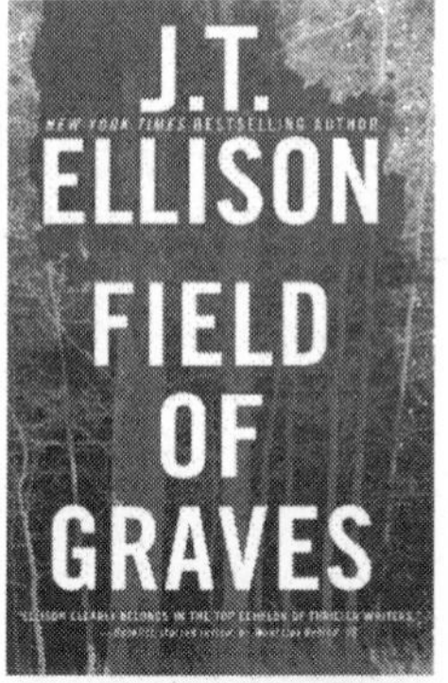

Turn the page
for excerpts from
their latest novels

Available from
Amazon,
Barnes & Noble
and Independent
Booksellers
thru
INDIEBOUND.org

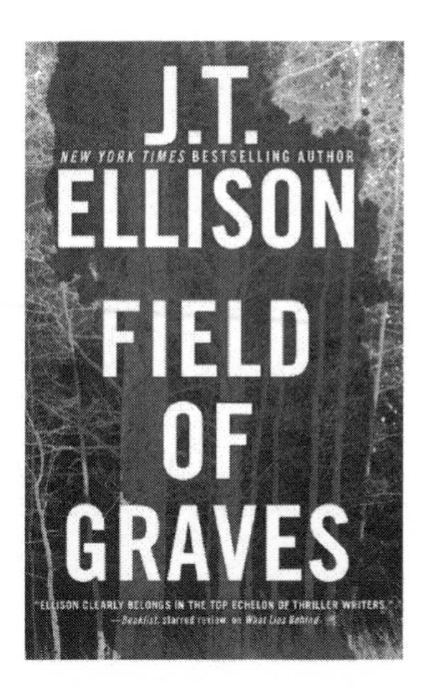

With FIELD OF GRAVES, *New York Times* bestselling author J.T. Ellison goes back to where it all began...

All of Nashville is on edge with a serial killer on the loose. A madman is trying to create his own end-of-days apocalypse and the cops trying to catch him are almost as damaged as the killer. Field of Graves reveals the origins of some of J.T. Ellison's most famous creations: the haunted Lieutenant Taylor Jackson; her blunt, exceptional best friend, medical examiner Dr. Samantha Owens; and troubled FBI profiler Dr. John Baldwin. Together, they race the clock and their own demons to find the killer before he claims yet another victim. This dark, thrilling and utterly compelling novel will have readers on the edge of their seats, and Ellison's fans will be delighted with the revelations about their favorite characters.

MIRA Books
a division of Harlequin
225 Duncan Mill Road
Toronto, Ontario M3B 3K9
Canada

ISBN-13: 9780778318927 (hardcover)
ISBN-13: 9780778330530 (paperback)
ISBN-13: 9781459294165 (ebook)

This book is a work of fiction. Any references to historical events, real people, or real places are used fictitiously. Other names, characters, places, and events are products of the author's imagination, and any resemblance to actual events or places or persons, living or dead, is entirely coincidental.

Prologue

Taylor picked up her portable phone for the tenth time in ten minutes. She hit Redial, heard the call connect and start ringing, then clicked the Off button and returned the phone to her lap. Once she made this call, there was no going back. Being right wouldn't make her the golden girl. If she were wrong—well, she didn't want to think about what could happen. Losing her job would be the least of her worries.

Damned if she did. Damned if she didn't.

She set the phone on the pool table and went down the stairs of her small two-story cabin. In the kitchen, she opened the door to the refrigerator and pulled out a Diet Coke. She laughed to herself. As if more caffeine would give her the courage to make the call. She should try a shot of whiskey. That always worked in the movies.

She snapped open the tab and stood staring out of her kitchen window. It had been dark for hours—the moon gone and the inky blackness outside her window impenetrable—but in an hour the skies would lighten. She would have to make a decision by then.

She turned away from the window and heard a loud crack. The lights went out. She jumped a mile, then giggled nervously, a hand to her chest to stop the sudden pounding.

Silly girl, she thought. *The lights go out all the time. There was a Nashville Electric Service crew on the corner when you drove in earlier; they must have messed up the line and a power surge caused the lights to blow. It happens every time NES works on the lines. Now stop it. You're a grown woman. You're not afraid of the dark.*

She reached into her junk drawer and groped for a flashlight. Thumbing the switch, she cursed softly when the light didn't shine. Batteries, where were the batteries?

She froze when she heard the noise and immediately went on alert, all of her senses going into overdrive. She strained her ears, trying to hear it again. Yes, there it was. A soft scrape off the back porch. She took a deep breath and sidled out of the kitchen, keeping close to the wall, moving lightly toward the back door. She brought her hand to her side and found nothing. Damn it. She'd left her gun upstairs.

The tinkling of breaking glass brought her up short.

The French doors leading into the backyard had been breached. It was too late to head upstairs and get the gun. She would have to walk right through the living room to get to the stairs. Whoever had just broken through her back door was not going to let her stroll on by. She started edging back toward the kitchen, holding her breath, as if that would help her not make any noise.

She didn't see the fist, only felt it crack against her jaw. Her eyes swelled with tears, and before she could react, the fist connected again. She spun and hit the wall face first. The impact knocked her breath out. Her lips cut on the edge of her teeth; she tasted blood. The intruder grabbed her as she started to slide down the wall. Yanked her to her feet and put his hands around her throat, squeezing hard.

Now she knew exactly where her attacker was, and she fought back with everything she had. She struggled against him, quickly realizing she was in trouble. He was stronger than her, bigger than her. And he was there to kill.

She went limp, lolled bonelessly against him, surprising

him with the sudden weight. He released one arm in response, and she took that moment to whirl around and shove with all her might. It created some space between them, enabling her to slip out of his grasp. She turned quickly but crashed into the slate end table. He was all over her. They struggled their way into the living room. She began to plan. Kicked away again.

Her attacker lunged after her. She used the sturdy side table to brace herself and whipped out her left arm in a perfect jab, aiming lower than where she suspected his chin would be. She connected perfectly and heard him grunt in pain. Spitting blood out of her mouth in satisfaction, she followed the punch with a kick to his stomach, heard the *whoosh* of his breath as it left his body. He fell hard against the wall. She spun away and leapt to the stairs. He jumped up to pursue her, but she was quicker. She pounded up the stairs as fast as she could, rounding the corner into the hall just as her attacker reached the landing. Her weapon was in its holster, on the bookshelf next to the pool table, right where she had left it when she'd gone downstairs for the soda. She was getting careless. She should never have taken it off her hip. With everything that was happening, she shouldn't have taken for granted that she was safe in her own home.

Her hand closed around the handle of the weapon. She pulled the Glock from its holster, whipped around to face the door as the man came tearing through it. She didn't stop to think about the repercussions, simply reacted. Her hand rose by instinct, and she put a bullet right between his eyes. His momentum carried him forward a few paces. He was only five feet from her, eyes black in death, when he dropped with a thud.

She heard her own ragged breathing. She tasted blood and raised a bruised hand to her jaw, feeling her lips and her teeth gingerly. Son of a bitch had caught her right in the jaw and loosened two molars. The adrenaline rush left her. She collapsed on the floor next to the lifeless body. She might have even slept for a moment.

The throbbing in her jaw brought her back. Morning was beginning to break, enough to see the horrible mess in front of her. The cat was sit-ting on the pool table, watching her curiously.

Rising, she took in the scene. The man was collapsed on her game room floor, slowly leaking blood on her Berber carpet. She peered at the stain.

That's going to be a bitch to get out.

She shook her head to clear the cobwebs. What an inane thing to say. Shock, she must be going into shock. How long had they fought? Had it been only five minutes? Half an hour? She felt as though she had struggled against him for days; her body was tired and sore. Never mind the blood caked around her mouth. She put her hand up to her face. Make that her nose too.

She eyed the man again. He was facedown and angled slightly to one side. She slipped her toes under his right arm and flipped him over with her foot. The shot was true; she could see a clean entry wound in his forehead. Reaching down out of habit, she felt for his carotid pulse, but there was nothing. He was definitely dead.

"Oh, David," she said. "You absolute idiot. Look what you've made me do."

Now the shit was absolutely going to hit the fan. It was time to make the call.

Chapter 1

Three months later
Nashville, Tennessee

Bodies, everywhere bodies, a field of graves, limbs and torsos and heads, all left above ground. The feeling of dirt in her mouth, grimy and thick; the whispers from the dead, long arms reaching for her as she passed through the carnage. Ghostly voices, soft and sibilant. "Help us. Why won't you help us?"

Taylor jerked awake, sweating, eyes wild and blind in the darkness. The sheets twisted around her body in a claustrophobic shroud, and she struggled to get them untangled. She squeezed her eyes shut, willed her breathing back to normal, trying to relax, to let the grisly images go. When she opened her eyes, the room was still dark but no longer menacing. Her screams had faded away into the silence. The cat jumped off the bed with a disgruntled meow in response to her thrashing.

She laid her head back on the pillow, swallowed hard, still unable to get a full breath.

Every damn night. She was starting to wonder if she'd ever sleep well again.

She wiped a hand across her face and looked at the clock:

6:10 a.m. The alarm was set for seven, but she wasn't going to get any more rest. She might as well get up and get ready for work. Go in a little early, see what horrors had captured the city overnight.

She rolled off the bed, trying hard to forget the dream. Showered, dressed, dragged on jeans and a black cashmere T-shirt under a black motorcycle jacket, stepped into her favorite boots. Put her creds in her pocket and her gun on her hip. Pulled her wet hair off her face and into a ponytail.

Time to face another day.

She was in her car when the call came. "Morning, Fitz. What's up?"

"Morning, LT. We have us a body at the Parthenon."

"I'll be right there."

* * * *

It might have become a perfect late autumn morning. The sky was busy, turning from white to blue as dawn rudely forced its way into day. Birds were returning from their mysterious nocturnal errands, greeting and chattering about the night's affairs. The air was clear and heavy, still muggy from the overnight heat but holding a hint of coolness, like an ice cube dropped into a steaming mug of coffee. The sky would soon shift to sapphire the way only autumn skies do, as clear and heavy as the precious stone itself.

The beauty of the morning was lost on Lieutenant Taylor Jackson, Criminal Investigation Division, Nashville Metro Police. She snapped her long body under the yellow crime scene tape and looked around for a moment. Sensed the looks from the officers around her. Straightened her shoulders and marched toward them.

Metro officers had been traipsing around the crime scene control area like it was a cocktail party, drinking coffee and chatting each other up as though they'd been apart for weeks, not hours. The grass was already littered with cups, cigarette butts, crumpled notebook paper, and at least one copy of the morning's sports section from *The Tennessean*. Taylor cursed silently; they knew better than this. One of these yahoos was going to inadvertently contaminate a crime scene one of these days, send in her team off on a wild goose chase. Guess whose ass would be in the proverbial sling then?

She stooped to grab the sports page, surreptitiously glanced at the headline regaling the Tennessee Titans' latest win, then crumpled it into a firm ball in her hands.

Taylor didn't know what information about the murder had leaked out over the air, but the curiosity factor had obviously kicked into high gear. An officer she recognized from another sector was cruising by to check things out, not wanting to miss out on all the fun. Media vans lined the street. Joggers pretending not to notice anything was happening nearly tripped trying to see what all the fuss was about. Exactly what she needed on no sleep: everyone willing to help, to get in and screw up her crime scene.

Striding toward the melee, she tried to tell herself that it wasn't their fault she'd been up all night. At least she'd had a shower and downed two Diet Cokes, or she would have arrested them all.

She reached the command post and pasted on a smile. "Mornin', kids. How many of you have dragged this crap through my crime scene?" She tossed the balled up paper at the closest officer.

She tried to keep her tone light, as if she were amused by their shenanigans, but she didn't fool anyone, and the levity disappeared from the gathering. The brass was on the scene, so all the fun had come to a screeching halt. Uniforms who didn't belong started to drift away, one or two giving Taylor a sideways glance. She ignored them, the way she ignored most things these days.

As a patrol officer, she'd kept her head down, worked her cases, and developed a reputation for being a straight shooter. Her dedication and clean work had been rewarded with promotion after promotion; she was in plainclothes at twenty-eight. She'd caught a nasty first case in Homicide—the kidnapping and murder of a young girl. She'd nailed the bastard who'd done it; Richard Curtis was on death row now. The case made the national news and sent her career into overdrive. She quickly became known for being a hard-hitting investigator and moved up the ranks from detective to lead to sergeant, until she'd been given the plum job she had now—homicide lieutenant.

If her promotion to lieutenant at the tender age of thirty-four had rankled some of the more traditional officers on the force, the death of David Martin—one of their own—made it ten times worse. There were always going to be cops who tried to make her life difficult; it was part of being a chick on the force, part of having a reputation. Taylor was tough, smart, and liked to do things her own way to get the job done. The majority of the men she worked with had great respect for her abilities. There were always going to be detractors, cops who whispered behind her back, but in Taylor's mind, success trumped rumor every time.

Then Martin had decided to ruin her life and nearly derailed her career in the process. She was still clawing her way back.

Taylor's second in command, Detective Pete Fitzgerald, lumbered toward her, the ever-present unlit cigarette hanging out of his mouth. He'd quit a couple of years before, after a minor heart attack, but kept one around to light in case of an emergency. Fitz had an impressive paunch; his belly reached Taylor before the rest of his body.

"Hey, LT. Sorry I had to drag you away from your beauty sleep." He looked her over, concern dawning in his eyes. "I was just kidding. What's up with you? You look like shit warmed over."

Taylor waved a hand in dismissal. "Didn't sleep. Aren't we supposed to have some sort of eclipse this morning? I think it's got me all out of whack."

Fitz took the hint and backed down. "Yeah, we are." He looked up quickly, shielding his eyes with his hand. "See, it's already started."

He was right. The moon was moving quickly across the sun, the crime scene darkening by the minute. "Eerie," she said.

He looked back at her, blinking hard. "No kidding. Remind me not to stare into the sun again."

"Will do. Celestial phenomenon aside, what do we have here?"

"Okay, darlin', here we go. We have a couple of lovebirds who decided to take an early morning stroll—found themselves a deceased Caucasian female on the Parthenon's steps. She's sitting up there pretty as you please, just leaning against the gate in front of the Parthenon doors like she sat down for a rest. Naked as a jaybird too, and very, very dead."

Taylor turned her gaze to the Parthenon. One of her favorite sites in Nashville, smack-dab in the middle of Centennial Park, the full-size replica was a huge draw for tourists and classicists alike. The statue of Athena inside was awe-inspiring. She couldn't count how many school field trips she'd been on here over the years. Leaving a body on the steps was one hell of a statement.

"Where are the witnesses?"

"Got the lovebirds separated, but the woman's having fits—we haven't been able to get a full statement. The scene's taped off. Traffic on West End has been blocked off, and we've closed all roads into and around Centennial Park. ME and her team have been here about fifteen minutes. Oh, and our killer was here at some point too." He grinned at her lopsidedly. "He dumped her sometime overnight, only the duckies and geese in the lake saw him. This is gonna be a bitch to canvass. Do you think we can admit 'AFLAC' as a statement in court?"

Taylor gave him a quick look and a perfunctory laugh, more amused at imagining Fitz waddling about like the duck from the insurance ads quacking than at his irreverent attitude. She knew better, but it did seem as if he was having a good time. Taylor understood that sometimes inappropriate attempts at humor were the only way a cop could make it through the day, so she chastised him gently. "You've got a sick sense of humor, Fitz." She sighed, turning off all personal thoughts, becoming a cop again. All business, all the time. That's what they needed to see from her.

"We'll probably have to go public and ask who was here last night and when, but I'm not holding my breath that we'll get anything helpful, so let's put it off for now."

He nodded in agreement. "Do you want to put up the chopper? Probably useless—whoever dumped her is long gone."

"I think you're right." She jerked her head toward the Parthenon steps. "What's he trying to tell us?"

Fitz looked toward the doors of the Parthenon, where the medical examiner was crouched over the naked body. His voice dropped, and he suddenly became serious. "I don't know, but this is going to get ugly, Taylor. I got a bad feeling."

Taylor held a hand up to cut him off. "C'mon, man, they're all ugly. It's too early to start spinning. Let's just get through the morning. Keep the frickin' media out of here—put 'em down in the duck shit if you have to. You can let them know which roads are closed so they can get the word out to their traffic helicopters, but that's it. Make sure the uniforms keep everyone off the tape. I don't want another soul in here until I have a chance to be fully briefed by all involved. Has the Park Police captain shown up yet?"

Fitz shook his head. "Nah. They've called him, but I haven't seen him."

"Well, find him, too. Make sure they know which end is up. Let's get the perimeter of this park searched, grid by grid, see if we find something. Get K-9 out here, let them do an article search. Since the roads are already shut off, tell them to expand the perimeter one thousand outside the borders of the park. I want to see them crawling around like ants at a picnic. I see any of them hanging in McDonald's before this is done, I'm kicking some butt."

Fitz gave her a mock salute. "I'm on it. When Sam determined she was dumped, I went ahead and called K-9, and pulled all the officers coming off duty. We may have an overtime situation, but I figured with your, um, finesse—" He snorted out the last word, and Taylor eyed him coolly.

"I'll handle it." She pushed her hair back from her face and reestablished her hurried ponytail. "Get them ready for all hell to break loose. I'm gonna go talk to Sam."

"Glad to serve, love. Now go see Sam, and let the rest of us grunts do our jobs. If you decide you want the whirlybird, give me a thumbs-up." He blew her a kiss and marched toward the command post, snapping his fingers at the officers to get their attention.

Turning toward the building, she caught a stare from one of the older patrols. His gaze was hostile, lip curled in a sneer. She gave him her most brilliant smile, making his scowl deepen. She broke off the look, shaking her head. She didn't have time to worry about politics right now.

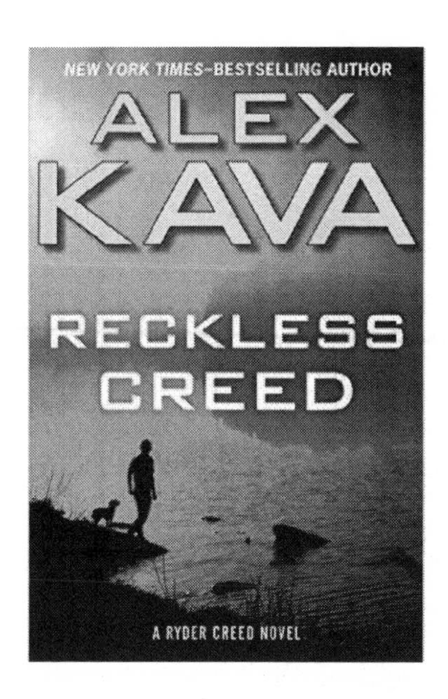

In the new edge-of-your-seat thriller from *New York Times* bestselling author Alex Kava, Ryder Creed, his K-9 search-and-rescue dogs, and FBI agent Maggie O'Dell find themselves at the center of a dire and mysterious case.

In Chicago, a young man jumps from his thirtieth-story hotel room; along the Missouri river, a hunter and his son stumble upon a lake whose surface is littered with snow geese, all of them dead; and in southern Alabama, Ryder Creed and his search-and-rescue dog Grace find the body of a young woman who went missing in the Conecuh National Forest, and it appears she filled her pockets with rocks and walked into the river. Before long Ryder Creed and FBI profiler Maggie O'Dell will discover the ominous connection among these mysterious deaths. What they find may be the most prolific killer the United States has ever known.

Chapter 1

Chicago

Tony Briggs coughed up blood, then wiped his mouth with his shirt-sleeve. This was bad. Although it was nothing he couldn't handle. He'd been through worse. Lots worse. But still, they didn't tell him he'd get this sick. He was beginning to think the bastards had double-crossed him.

He tapped out, "fine mess I got myself into," on his cell phone and hit SEND before he changed his mind.

The text message wasn't part of his instructions. Not part of the deal. He didn't care. So what if the watchers found out. What could they do to him now? He already felt like crap. They couldn't make him feel much worse.

He tossed the phone into the garbage can along with the few brochures he'd picked up throughout the day. His itinerary read like a sight-seeing family vacation. Or in his case, something presented by one of those make-a-wish charities – one final trip, all expenses paid.

He laughed at that and ended up in a coughing fit. Blood sprayed the flat screen TV and even the wall behind. He didn't like leaving the mess for the hotel housekeeping staff. But it was a little too late for that. Especially since his instructions included touching everything he could throughout the day. The list rattled in his head: light switches, elevator buttons, restaurant menus, remote control, and escalator handrails.

Earlier that morning at the McDonald's—before the cough, just before the fever spiked and he still had a bit of bravado along with an appetite—he felt his first tinge of apprehension. He'd taken his tray and stopped at the condiment counter.

Touch as many surfaces as possible.

That's what he'd been told. Germs could live on a hard surface for up to eighteen hours. He may have screwed up a lot of things in his life but he could still follow instructions.

That's what he'd been thinking when he felt a tap on his elbow.

"Hey, mister, could you please hand me two straws?"

The kid was six, maybe seven with nerdy glasses, the thick black frames way too big for his face. He kept shoving at them, the motion second nature. The kid reminded Tony immediately of his best friend, Jason. They had grown up together since they were six years old. Same schools. Same football team. Joined the Army together. Even came back from Afghanistan, both screwed up in one way or another. Tony was the athlete. Jason was the brains. Smart and pushy even at six. But always following Tony around.

Old four eyes.

"Whadya doing now?" was Jason's favorite catch phrase.

In grade school they went through a period where Jason mimicked everything Tony did. In high school the kid bulked up just so he could be on the football team, right alongside Tony. In the back of his mind he knew Jason probably joined the Army only because Tony wanted to. And look where it got them.

Tony shoved at the guilt. And suddenly at that moment he found himself hoping that Jason never found out what a coward he really was.

"Mister," the kid waited with his hand outstretched.

Tony caught himself reaching for the damned straw dispenser then stopped short, fingertips inches away.

"Get your own damned straws," he told the kid. "You're not crippled."

Then he turned and left without even getting his own straw or napkin. Without touching a single thing on the whole frickin' condiment counter. In fact, he took his tray and walked out, shouldering the door open so he wouldn't have to touch it either. He dumped the tray and food in a nearby trashcan. The kid had unnerved him so much it took him almost an hour to move on.

Now back in his hotel room, sweat trickled down his face. He wiped at his forehead with the same sleeve he'd used on his mouth.

The fever was something he'd expected. The blurred vision was a surprise.

No, it was more than blurred vision. The last hour or so he knew he'd been having hallucinations. He thought he saw one of his old drill sergeants in the lobby of the John Hancock building. But he'd been too nauseated from the observatory to check it out. Still, he remembered to touch every single button before he got out of the elevator. Nauseated and weak-kneed.

And he was embarrassed.

His mind might not be what it once was thanks to what the doctors called traumatic brain injury, but he was proud that he'd kept his body lean and strong when so many of his buddies had come back without limbs. Now the muscle fatigue set in and it actually hurt to breathe.

Just then Tony heard a click in the hotel room. It came from somewhere behind him. It sounded like the door.

The room's entrance had a small alcove for the minibar and coffee maker. He couldn't see the door without crossing the room.

"Is anybody there?" he asked as he stood up out of the chair.

Was he hallucinating again or had a shadow moved?

Suddenly everything swirled and tipped to the right. He leaned against the room service cart. He'd ordered it just like his watchers had instructed him to do when he got back to his room. Nevermind that he hadn't been able to eat a thing. Even the scent of fresh strawberries made his stomach roil.

No one was there.

Maybe the fever was making him paranoid. It certainly made him feel like he was burning up from the inside. He needed to cool down. Get some fresh air.

Tony opened the patio door and immediately shivered. The small cement balcony had a cast-iron railing, probably one of the original fixtures that the hotel decided to keep when renovating—something quaint and historic.

The air felt good. Cold against his sweat-drenched body, but good. Made him feel alive. And he smiled at that. Funny how being this sick could make him feel so alive. He'd come close to being killed in Afghanistan several times, knew the exhilaration afterwards.

He stepped out into the night. His head was still three pounds too heavy, but the swirling sensation had eased a bit. And he could breathe finally without hacking up blood.

Listening to the rumble and buzz of the city below he realized if he wanted to, there'd be nothing to this. He had contemplated his own death many times since coming home but never once had he imagined this.

Suddenly he realized it'd be just like stepping out of a C-130.

Only without a parachute.

Nineteen stories made everything look like a miniature world below. Matchbox cars. The kind he and Jason had played with. Fought over. Traded. Shared.

And that's when his second wave of nausea hit him.

Maybe he didn't have to finish this. He didn't even care any more whether they paid him or not. Maybe it wasn't too late to get to an emergency room. They could probably give him something. Then he'd just go home. There were easier ways to make a few bucks.

But as he started to turn around he felt a shove. Not the wind. Strong hands. A shadow. His arms flailed trying to restore his balance.

Another shove.

His fingers grabbed for the railing but his body was already tipping. The metal dug into the small of his back. His vision blurred with streaks of light. His ears filled with the echo of a wind tunnel. The cold air surrounded him.

No second chances. He was already falling.

Chapter 2

Conecuh National Forest
Just north of the Alabama/Florida state line

Ryder Creed's T-shirt stuck to his back. His hiking boots felt like cement blocks, caked with red clay. The air grew heavier, wet and stifling. The scent of pine mixed with the gamy smell of exertion from both man and dog. This deep in the woods even the birds were different, the drilling of the red-cockaded woodpecker the only sound to interrupt the continuous buzz of mosquitoes.

He was grateful for the long-sleeved shirt and the kerchief around his neck as well as the one around Grace's. The fabric had been soaked in a special concoction that his business partner, Hannah, had mixed up, guaranteed to repel bugs. Hannah joked that one more ingredient and maybe it'd even keep them safe from vampires.

In a few hours it would be nighttime in the forest, and deep in the sticks, as they called it, on the border of Alabama and Florida, there were enough reasons to drive a man to believe in vampires. The kudzu climbed and twisted up the trees so thick it looked like green netting. There were places the sunlight couldn't squeeze down through the branches.

Their original path was quickly becoming overgrown. Thorny vines grabbed at Creed's pantlegs, and he worried they were ripping into Grace's short legs. He was already second-guessing bringing the Jack Russell terrier instead of one of his bigger dogs, but Grace was the best air scent dog he had in a pack of dozens. And she was scampering along en-joying the adventure, making her way easily through the tall longleaf pines that grew so close Creed had to sidestep in spots.

They had less than an hour until sunset, and yet the federal agent from Atlanta was still questioning Creed.

"You don't think you need more than the one dog?"

Agent Lawrence Taber had already remarked several times about how small Grace was, and that she was "kind of scrawny." Creed heard him whisper to Sheriff Wylie that he was "pretty sure Labs or German shepherds were the best trackers."

Creed was used to it. He knew that neither he nor his dogs were what most law enforcement officers expected. He'd been training and handling dogs for over seven years. His business, K9 CrimeScents, had a waiting list for his dogs. Yet people expected him to be older, and his dogs to be bigger.

Grace was actually one of his smallest dogs, a scrappy brown-and-white Jack Russell terrier. Creed had discovered her abandoned at the end of his long driveway. When he found her she was skin and bones but sagging where she had recently been nursing puppies. Locals had gotten into the habit of leaving their unwanted dogs at the end of Creed's fifty-acre property. It wasn't the first time he had seen a female dog dumped and punished when the owner was simply too cheap to get her spayed.

Hannah didn't like that people took advantage of Creed's soft heart. But what no one—not even Hannah—understood was that the dogs Creed rescued were some of his best air scent trackers. Skill was only a part of the training. Bonding with the trainer was another. His rescued dogs trusted him unconditionally and were loyal beyond measure. They were eager to learn and anxious to please. And Grace was one of his best.

"Working multiple dogs at the same time can present problems," he finally told the agent. "Competition between the dogs. False alerts. Over-lapping grids. Believe me, one dog will be more than sufficient."

Creed kept his tone matter of fact for Grace's sake. Emotion runs down the leash. Dogs could detect their handler's mood, so Creed always tried to keep his temper in check even when guys like Agent Taber started to piss him off.

He couldn't help wonder why Tabor was here, but he kept it to himself. Creed wasn't law enforcement. He was hired to do a job and had no interest in questioning jurisdiction or getting involved in the pissing contests that local and federal officials often got into.

"I can't think she'd run off this far," Sheriff Wylie said.

He was talking about the young woman they were looking for. The reason they were out here searching. But now Creed realized the sheriff was starting to question his judgment, too, even though the two of them had worked together plenty of times.

Creed ignored both men as best he could and concentrated on Grace. He could hear her breathing getting more rapid. She started to hold her nose higher and he tightened his grip on the leash. She had definitely entered a scent cone but Creed had no idea if it was secondary or primary. All he could smell was the river, but that wasn't what had Grace's attention.

"How long has she been gone?" Creed asked Sheriff Wylie.

"Since the night before last."

Creed had been told that Izzy Donner was nineteen, a recovering drug addict who was getting her life back on track. She had enrolled in college part-time and was even looking forward to a trip to Atlanta she had planned with friends. Creed still wasn't quite sure why her family had panicked. A couple nights out of touch didn't seem out of ordinary for a teenager.

"Tell me again why you think she ran off into the forest. Are you sure she wasn't taken against her will?"

Seemed like a logical reason that a federal agent might be involved if the girl had been taken. The two men exchanged a glance. Creed suspected they were withholding information from him.

"Why would it matter?" Tabor finally asked. "If your dog is any good it should still be able to find her, right?"

"It would matter because there'd be another person's scent."

"We had a tip called in," Wylie admitted but Tabor shot him a look and cut him off from saying anything else.

Before Creed could push for more, Grace started straining at the end of the leash. Her breathing had increased, her nose and whiskers twitched. He knew she was headed for the river.

"Slow down a bit, Grace," he told her.

Slow down was something a handler didn't like telling his dog. But sometimes the drive could take over and send a dog barreling through dangerous terrain. He'd heard of working dogs scraping their pads raw, so focused and excited about finding the scent that would reward them.

Grace kept pulling. Creed's long legs were moving fast to keep up. The tangle of vines threatened to trip him while Grace skipped between them, jumping over fallen branches and straining at the end of her leash. He focused on keeping up with her and not letting go.

Only now did Creed notice that Agent Tabor and Sheriff Wylie were trailing farther behind. He didn't glance back but could hear their voices becoming more muffled, interspersed with some curses as they tried to navigate the prickly underbrush.

Finally Grace slowed down. Then she stopped. But the little dog was still frantically sniffing the air. Creed could see and hear the river five feet away. He watched Grace and waited. Suddenly the dog looked up to find his eyes and stared at him.

This was their signal. Creed knew the dog wasn't trying to determine what direction to go next, nor was she looking to him for instructions. Grace was telling him she had found their target. That she knew exactly where it was but she didn't want to go any closer.

Something was wrong.

"What is it?" Sheriff Wylie asked while he and Tabor approached, trying to catch their breaths and keep a safe distance.

"I think she's in the water," Creed said.

"What do you mean she's in the water," Tabor asked.

But Wylie understood. "Oh crap."

"Grace, stay," Creed told the dog and dropped the leash.

He knew he didn't need the command. The dog was spooked and it made Creed's stomach start to knot up.

He maneuvered his way over the muddy clay of the riverbank, hold-in onto tree branches to keep from sliding. He didn't know that Wylie was close behind until he heard the older man's breath catch at the same time that Creed saw the girl's body.

Her eyes stared up as if she were watching the clouds. The girl's windbreaker was still zipped up and had ballooned out, causing her up-per body to float while the rest of her lay on the sandy bottom. This part of Blackwater River was only about three feet deep. Though tea-colored, the water was clear. And even in the fading sunlight Creed could see that the girl's pockets were weighted down.

"Son of bitch," he heard Wylie say from behind. "Looks like she loaded up her pockets with rocks and walked right into the river."

Detectives Micki Dare and Zach Harris are back in TRIPLE SIX, their second adventure in Erica Spindler's supernatural thriller series The Lightkeepers.

It's been three months since that night - the night that Micki almost died. Physically, she's healed but the nightmares remain, and she can't shake the feeling that more happened that night than Zach is telling her. The only thing she can do is try to carry on as normal and solve the latest case she and Zach have been assigned to.

A string of brutal home invasions are rocking New Orleans and the families targeted seemingly have nothing in common. Why were these victims chosen? The deeper Micki and Zach go into the case, the more they realize something isn't right. There's something familiar about the person doing this - and it's a familiarity Micki has been trying to forget. Suddenly, this case is hitting too close to home and Micki has to decide if she really wants to learn the truth about that night…

Prologue

New Orleans, Louisiana
Monday, July 22nd
3:00 p.m.

Lost Angel Ministries. Zach Harris stood at the wrought iron gate, gazing at the sign as it swayed in the breeze. The iron fence circled the property, a Victorian home from days gone by, repurposed into a center that helped lost and disenfranchised youth. Youth who were special. Very.

The front door opened and a teenager darted out, calling 'bye over her shoulder. She was small with a spiky, pixie haircut, the spikes dyed Irish green. She met his eyes as she reached the gate. Beautiful eyes. A brilliant green that matched her hair.

She was one of them. Lightkeeper.

Or like him, a mutation of one.

"Hey," she said, slipping past him.

"Hey," he responded back, and headed through the gate and up the walk. It felt weird, thinking of himself that way. A light being enrobed in human flesh? Sent to guide the human race, steer it toward good. Mortal angels in a life or death battle with an ancient evil?

It felt like total bullshit. It pissed him off. He might not want to buy in, but at this point, he didn't have a choice. Like it or not, his eyes had been opened.

From the neutral ground behind him came the rumble of the streetcar. He glanced over his shoulder at it, bright, shiny red, windows shut tight to keep the heat out. He reached the door, looked directly at the security camera and was buzzed in.

Eli met him in the foyer. He looked no worse for wear, as if saving lives and battling the forces of darkness had the rejuvenating properties of a spa day.

"Zach, buddy—" He clapped him on the back. "—great to see you. Come, they're in the conference room."

They started in that direction. Eli turned his extraordinary gaze on him. "You've been to the hospital and seen Michaela?"

"Left just a little bit ago."

"How is she?"

"Healing quickly. Very."

"I do good work."

The cockiness annoyed the crap out of him. "She says she remembers being surrounded by a beautiful, healing light. Like being wrapped in an angel's wings."

Eli stopped and cocked his head. "Did she? That's curious. And what did you tell her?"

"That she had lost a lot of blood, was in shock or hallucinating."

"Good. Here we are."

"Wait." Zach laid a hand on his arm, stopping him. "I thought you said she wouldn't remember anything."

"That's why it's curious." He smiled. "I don't think it's anything you need to worry about."

Famous last words, Zach thought and stepped into the conference room. Only two at the table: Parker and Professor Truebell.

"Zachary." Truebell stood and held out his hand, smiling.

Zach took it. "Professor."

"No worse for wear, I see."

"Tell that to every muscle, joint and bone in my body." He indicated the four of them. "We're it?"

"For today, yes."

"No Angel?"

"She's not ready."

The comment rankled. More secrets. More need-to-know bullshit. "I see nothing's changed since the last time I sat across this table from you."

The elfin Truebell shook his head. "Everything's changed, Zachary. Sit. Please."

He did. Parker spoke up. "No hello for me, Zach?"

He looked at him, not masking his anger. "I may have to work with you, Special Agent Parker, but I don't have to like you. And I sure as hell don't have to respect you."

Parker leaned back in his chair and folded his arms across his chest. "You don't think that's a little harsh? And formal, considering we're family?"

"You lied to me. Manipulated me. You kept your real identity a secret from me." He arched his eyebrows. "No. Not too harsh. And as for the last part, I don't have anyone's word on that but yours."

"You'll come around."

"Don't count on it." He shifted his attention back to Truebell. "Why am I here today?"

"You know why."

"Do I?"

"Are you in," Truebell asked, "or out?"

He wished he could say he was out, shake this whole experience off, and go back to the life he had known before. But that life was gone forever. "Saturday made a believer out of me."

He nodded. "You know it's destructive power now. You understand our urgency."

His head filled with the memory of that power turned on him, his helplessness against it. "Yes."

"And now you know ours as well."

The joining of the Lightkeepers. The explosion of light. The howl of rage as the Dark Bearer had been forced out.

Darkness cannot exist in the light, Zach.

But it could put up a hell of a fight.

"How many of us were there that night," Zach asked. "A dozen?"

"More. Fourteen."

"Fourteen to overcome one? I suppose you've noticed those odds suck for us."

"They do, indeed. So, Zachary, now that you're a believer and you know the odds, are you with us?"

He held the professor's gaze. "I'm in. For now."

Professor Truebell smiled slightly. "Not quite the gung-ho response I'd hoped for, but it'll do for now. One last thing—" He folded his hands on the table and leaned toward Zach. "—I have to have your word. You'll do what you need to do, concerning Michaela?"

He hated this. She was his partner. Secrets put her in harm's way.

No, Zach. They make her safer.

He looked at Eli. *Get out of my head.*

You have to trust us.

I trust her.

"Zachary? Your answer."

"Yes. I'll tell her nothing of the Lightkeepers and nothing of the true nature of the events of that night."

"You won't regret it."

He regretted it already. "What's next?"

"We wait."

"For what?"

"The Dark Bearer's return."

J.T. ELLISON'S BOOKS

STANDALONE THRILLERS
LIE TO ME (available September 5, 2017)
NO ONE KNOWS

A Brit in the FBI Series with Catherine Coulter
1 - THE FINAL CUT
2 - THE LOST KEY
3 - THE END GAME
4 – THE DEVIL'S TRIANGLE (available March 14, 2017)

Lieutenant Taylor Jackson Series
0 – FIELD OF GRAVES
1 - ALL THE PRETTY GIRLS
2 - 14
3 - JUDAS KISS
4 - THE COLD ROOM
5 - THE IMMORTALS
6 - SO CLOSE THE HAND OF DEATH
7 - WHERE ALL THE DEAD LIE

Dr. Samantha Owens Series
1 - A DEEPER DARKNESS
2 - EDGE OF BLACK
3 - WHEN SHADOWS FALL
4 - WHAT LIES BEHIND

Available via Two Tales Press
THE FIRST DECADE: A Short Story Collection

Novellas with Erica Spindler and Alex Kava
(Featuring Taylor Jackson short stories)
SLICES OF NIGHT ("Blood Sugar Baby")
STORM SEASON ("Whiteout")

ALEX KAVAS'S BOOKS

THE RYDER CREED SERIES (In order)
Breaking Creed
Silent Creed
Reckless Creed
Lost Creed (available September 2017)

The Maggie O'Dell Series (In order)
A Perfect Evil
Split Second
The Soul Catcher
At The Stroke of Madness
A Necessary Evil
Exposed
Black Friday
Damaged
Hotwire
Fireproof
Stranded
Before Evil (available July 2017)

STANDALONE THRILLERS
One False Move
Whitewash

Original eBooks
A Breath of Hot Air (with Patricia A. Bremmer)

Novellas with Erica Spindler and Alex Kava
Slices of Night
Storm Season

Available via Prairie Wind Publishing
Off the Grid (A Maggie O'Dell Short Story Collection)

ERICA SPINDLER'S BOOKS

THE LIGHTKEEPER'S SERIES (In order)
The Final Seven
Triple Six

STANDALONES
The First Wife
Justice for Sara
Wishing Moon
Fortune
Watch Me Die
Dead Run
Blood Vines
Bone Cold
Break Neck
Forbidden Fruit
In Silence
See Jane Die
Red
Last Known Victim
Copy Cat
Killer Takes All
Shocking Pink
Cause for Alarm
All Fall Down
Chances Are

Novellas with J.T. Ellison and Alex Kava
Slices of Night
Storm Season

Connect with the Authors Online:

Erica Spindler
Website: http://www.ericaspindler.com/
Facebook: https://www.facebook.com/EricaSpindler
Twitter: https://twitter.com/EricaSpindler
Instagram:
https://www.instagram.com/erica.spindler.author/

J.T. Ellison
Website: http://jtellison.com/
Facebook: https://www.facebook.com/JTEllison14/
Twitter: https://twitter.com/thrillerchick
Instagram: https://www.instagram.com/jt_thrillerchick/

Alex Kava
Website: http://www.alexkava.com/
Facebook: https://www.facebook.com/alexkava.books
Twitter: https://twitter.com/alexkava_author

A Note from the Publisher

First of all, I want to thank you for reading *STORM SEASONS—One Storm. Three Novellas.* If you have enjoyed it I would be grateful if you would write a review. It doesn't have to be long—a few words would make a huge difference, in helping readers discover new authors for the first time.

I also know that J.T., Alex, and Erica would love to hear from you. Please find them on all the social media sites and get in on the conversations on their personal websites. Currently they are working on future books for your enjoyment.

Keep reading!

Deb Carlin

Made in the USA
San Bernardino, CA
27 December 2017